# Anjali's Story:
# My Magical Lip balm Adventure

Written by Preethi Nair

Illustrated by Amrina Rosyada
& Preethi Nair

First published in Great Britain in 2021
by Kiss The Frog Press
Copyright © 2021 by Preethi Nair

FIRST EDITION

The right of Preethi Nair to be identified as the
author has been asserted.

ISBN: 978-1-9989972-0-6

A CIP catalogue for this book is available from
the British Library.

This is a work of fiction. Names, places, events and
incidents are either the products of the author's
imagination or used fictitiously.

Any resemblance to actual persons, living or dead, is
purely coincidental.

Also available as an ebook

Typeset by Tiger Media

www.monsterlifelessons.com

For Anjali and for you, reader.

Everything happens on the inside first – in your imagination.

So, dream big and then dream bigger...

# Chapter 1
# The "Fff" Problem

I'm Anjali. I'm ten years old and I have a problem – chapped lips! Now, I know this might not sound like a big problem but it was turning into one. Like the snowball effect – you know when something so small can turn into an avalanche. So here's how it started: when it was cold, my lips would turn bright red and I would lick them constantly and start blurting a "ff and a ff and a ff". The "fff"s were a quiet whisper but Mum would say, "Anjali, please, not that again, just go and put on some lip balm." The problem was I didn't like any of the lip balms and I know I shouldn't have done this, but I just pretended to put lip balm on and continued with my calling out "fff"s silently.

Okay, let's go back to the beginning: I haven't told you the whole truth. I mean, I do have chapped lips but my "ff and a ff" problem started straight after my ammamma (grandma) died. I'm not sure why it happens, it just does and it was getting louder and more embarrassing, just like the growing snowball. Imagine, just erupting into a "ff and a ff and a ff" when you're nervous! I haven't told anyone not even Leyla, my BFF (Best Friend Forever). Leyla worries about absolutely everything and I didn't want her to start worrying about me too.

Then one day something happened to make the "fff"s ten times worse. Our class teacher, the lovely Miss Hawthorne, disappeared and nobody told us where she went or when she would be back. Shilpa Bandera, one of the girls in our class, said she ran off after auditioning for *The X Factor*, Rita said that she got married and Leyla worried that she might be ill. Mr D'Souza, our head teacher, said she was taking some time off and that we would be getting a supply teacher.

Anyway, the supply teacher's name – wait for it – was Mr Shutgun. The class did their normal thing when a supply teacher comes along and that was to misbehave. Simon Peters began by asking where his shotgun was. Mr Shutgun must have heard this joke a thousand times but instead of brushing it off with a laugh, Mr Shutgun gave Simon

detention right away. The class gasped and so nobody dared make a comment about his odd bow tie or his twirly moustache and beard, which looked like they belonged on a circus ringmaster.

"Right, open up your maths books, 5H. We're doing bar graphs," he commanded. Nobody moaned or shouted out and we did as we were instructed. He began explaining but because his voice was soporific (I've just learned this word and it means something that sends you to sleep), I began daydreaming about my ammamma and missed most of what he had said so when it was time to draw the bar graphs, well, mine were all over the place. He strode around the classroom inspecting our work and when he came near me, my heart began thumping.

Standing over my shoulder, he pointed his long, narrow finger at my page and announced, "This work is utterly ridiculous."

I wanted the seat to swallow me but all I could manage was a "ff and a ff and a ff" and it wasn't a whisper. The class started to laugh and the snowball gathered pace until it felt like I had been hit by a huge avalanche!

"Silence," he shouted at the class. He turned back to me and in a kinder tone began saying, "Well, when I meant ridiculous, I mean, it could be much better. It's actually not that bad." He corrected himself because I think he knew that I was going to cry.

And trust me, I wanted to cry because right then, I felt a dark spell had been cast and to stop myself from crying, I bit my chapped lip and it started to bleed.

Some teachers don't realise it but they have magical powers and should really be careful about what they say. Some use them for good, but others, not so much. So from that moment, every time I saw a maths question, my mind went blank. Oh, and then Lockdown happened and home-schooling started and it was a complete disaster. Well, at first it was fun because me and my brothers thought it was a bit of a holiday but then after the second week, my "fff"s were flying all over the place. My little brothers were running about, messing around and Mum couldn't get them to sit still and me, well, I couldn't do ANY of the maths, NONE OF IT! And my mum, who is normally really cool, began shouting at us. Everybody cried.

Mum tried her best to help me by showing me fractions using apples and oranges but even that didn't help. We watched *Numberock* together on the internet but no, that didn't work either. She kept asking me what the problem was and that she couldn't help me if I didn't tell her but I couldn't. I just couldn't. My "ffs" seemed to be getting worse, I couldn't hide them and I started pasting on lip balm to solve it but no amount of lip balm could help.

"Anjali," Mum said enthusiastically one evening as she was cooking dinner. "Look at this pie. How many slices do you think we could get out of it?"

"Ten," I replied.

"I think so too. How many slices do you think we could each eat?"

In my family there are five of us: me, my mum, my dad, my little brother Alfonso

(Sons), who is six, and Almendro (Mendy), who is four. They are really cute but sometimes can be a pain – well, Sons can. It's just that he thinks he can do everything that I can. And clearly, he can't, because I'm ten and he's only six.

That pie question was easy. It was ten divided by two. But as soon as I thought about it, my mind went blank – brain freeze – and I started to panic and my "fff"s came out.

Mum put the pie quickly in the oven, wiped her hands and sat down with me.

"It's okay, Anjali. I know you know the answer. What happened to make you scared of numbers? Please tell me and I promise we can sort it out."

Then I started to cry. I told her about Mr Shutgun and how he said my work was ridiculous and how I no longer found maths fun but boring – well, not even boring but SCARY! Every time I read a maths problem it started to scare me and then my brain would tell me I couldn't do it.

"It'll be okay," Mum replied, hugging me.

"There's always a solution."

Mum uses lots of sayings: "Every saucepan has a lid", "Every cloud has a silver lining", you name it, she's got a saying for it. Then Mum got a funny look on her face and as quick as a flash, like she had this massive brainwave, she said, "Anjali, if you could set up any business in the world, what would it be?"

"A business?"

"Yes, a business, something that you could make and sell."

That was really easy because me and my BFF Leyla have talked about this loads. We both love nature and we said we would start a flower shop but then Leyla, who worries about ABSOLUTELY everything, worried about how we would get the flowers – we couldn't just pick them from people's gardens and what would happen if we couldn't sell them and then we would have to watch them die!

I'd suggested seeds to Leyla. We could send people seeds to grow their own flowers or send them as gifts to other people. We never really got started because we forgot about the idea but now Mum was asking me.

"Seeds!" I blurted out.

"Seeds might be a bit complicated," Mum replied anxiously. Mum is not that into gardening especially after my ammamma accidentally stabbed Mum's foot with the garden fork. Mum was helping her plant tomatoes, Ammamma was chatting away and wasn't really concentrating and BANG, the fork went into Mum's wellington boot. Luckily she was wearing those boots and not her open-toe sandals, which she often does. Mum had to go to the hospital and hobbled around for weeks.

My dad is really the gardening expert in our family. He loves herbs and plants but I'm not sure he would have time to help me set up a seed business because now he has to be on Zoom calls all day long. When he does have time, he takes us on nature walks or to play outside and during Lockdown, I learned to cycle with my dad on the road. He tried taking the three of us out but it was a TOTAL disaster as Sons kept crashing into people and Mendy was crying. So now he takes the boys out on their own and I don't get to go as much.

"Any other business ideas, Anjali?" Mum asked.

"Well, how about making lip balm?" I suggested.

"Great idea!" she replied. "Let's do it. Let's make lip balm from scratch."

You might think that it's really cool to have a mum that says yes to ideas and just does it but let me explain, my mum is forever coming up with ideas. Some of them are WEIRD – like once there was a hole in the sleeve of her pyjama top and she put her thumb through it and said that we could start a fashion trend called the Glovejama!

Other times, she starts something but gets it half-finished or something goes wrong. There was the candle making, but she almost burned down the house. There was the making clay badges for all the relatives at Christmas – but she left the clay in the oven for too long so that the house smelled awful, like a poisonous smell that gave me and my brothers a headache for days. Then, when we tried making the badges that had been left in the oven for too long, they began to crumble. The ones we managed to save, we stuck magnets on, which all fell off and broke – that was the feedback from most of the relatives. Then there was cake making – I won't even begin... The list is endless.

Mum interrupted my memories of the latest disaster. "If we make lip balms, do you want to be in charge?"

In charge? In charge? Of course! I am never in charge of anything exciting – only loading the dishwasher and sometimes keeping an eye on my brothers.

I had a massive smile.

"Mum, can this just be our project?" Don't get me wrong, I do love my brothers but very, very rarely do I get to do stuff with my mum on my own.

"If that's what you want," she replied.

"And... can the lip balms be organic?" This is a new word I have learned too. 'Organic' means sort of natural with no chemicals (this was so as not to poison the house again with poisonous fumes). Also, do you know how many chemicals go into our body? Everything has chemicals. Did you know that the average household product has sixty-two chemicals and the average beauty product has more than this (I'm not sure how much more but I know it's more). What happens to the environment with all these chemicals? Leyla was worried and this was something I began to worry about too.

Mum sat down. "Let's do it, Anjali. Let's make a business plan."

Organic Lip Balm business

1. All natural ingredients.

2. Help people have smooth lips so they don't crack and then have a problem with their "fff s"

3. Make some money and give some money to charity

4. Have fun and spend time together

This was what our plan looked like. Drawn in an old notebook, it was very simple.

"So you are going to give a percentage of what you make to charity?" Mum asked.

"A percentage?"

"Yes, an amount – say 5 per cent, 10 per cent, 20 per cent. You decide."

It was then that I froze. Hang on a minute, was this a maths problem?

"Percentages? Is that maths, Mum?"

"Yes, darling," she said calmly, and do you know what she did? She tipped over the whole cutlery drawer on the table.

"There are a hundred pieces on this table. 'Per cent' means 'out of a hundred'. Now imagine you make one hundred pounds..."

One hundred pounds? Was she serious? Would we make £100?

"And," she continued, "you decide to give 10 per cent to charity. How much would you give?"

My mind just went blank.

"Don't worry, Anjali, I just want to show you how maths can be fun again."

Aha! So she had a cunning plan to get me to like maths again and what she didn't know at the time was that my cunning plan was to get her to finish things properly and so together our business of making lip balm was born.

# Stuff I've Learned

A business plan can be really simple, it's just an idea for your business and what you want to achieve.

"Percentage" means "out of a hundred". That's as far as I got!

# Chapter 2
# Inspirational People

People sometimes create businesses to solve problems. I wanted to try and be as eco-friendly as possible and so I looked up people who set up their businesses to make the world an eco-friendly place. They are known as eco-entrepreneurs.

Here are some grown-ups I found that are doing some cool things:

1. Jenny Costa – Rubies in the Rubble. (I love this name because I just imagine treasure in dirt so I think

a good name is important.) Jenny was shocked by the amount of food waste that came from fruit and vegetable markets in London. According to Jenny, there is about 7.2 million tonnes of food waste every year (that's like 6 million hippos). Her mission was to reduce some of it so she made a range of chutneys, ketchup and mayonnaise with the leftovers and began selling them. Ammamma would have loved this. She was into making chutneys but she just used to give them away.

I picked this next one because I thought it was really funny:

2. Simon Griffiths, Danny Alexander and Jehan Ratnatunga. Wait for it... They set up a company called – Who Gives a Crap! Who Gives a Crap makes toilet paper from a range of recycled materials and also bamboo which is supposed to be really

eco-friendly. They give 50 per cent of their profits to charities that install toilets and sewage systems in developing countries because they found out that 2.3 billion people don't have access to a toilet. Fifty per cent – I think that's a lot, like half of all their profits?

Then there was the incredible Mrs Marston (couldn't find a picture of her) but OMG Mrs Marston!

3. Mrs Marston set up an organic skincare company called – Mrs Marston's Magical Creams after spending time with tribes in the jungles of Borneo and the Amazon Rainforest. In 1966, she crashed her biplane in the jungles of Borneo. How did she get to fly a biplane? What was she doing there? Where was Borneo? (I had to look this up – it's in South East Asia.) I couldn't find out any more information about her but wait for it, after making

millions, she gave it all away to help conserve rainforests around the world and to stop them from being cut down. WOW!

I was so inspired by her that I wrote to ask her for her advice for setting up a business. I wrote her a letter because I wanted to impress her with my neatest handwriting. I have just got my pen licence – it took me years to get it. (Some of the kids in my class like Mark, Krishna and Coco got it in Year 2! I mean, Year 2??)

Dear Mrs Marston,
My name is Anjali. I am ten years old and I would really like to help save the planet just like you. I am EXTREMELY inspired by you (I have just read about you on the internet) and think you are ABSOLUTELY AMAZING!!!!
There are so many things that I want to ask you. What was it like in the jungles of Borneo? How did you survive your plane crash? What were the tribe like? We are learning about the Amazon Rainforest now. I mean not right now but it would be wonderful to find out what it

was really like in a rainforest.

It would be my absolute dream to meet you.

Yours sincerely,
Anjali

~~P.S. What was it like to be rich? Did you travel in first class? And what did it feel like to give away millions?~~

Mum had to help me with the "yours sincerely" bit as I never know what the rule is. Also, Mum asked me to take out the P.S. bit about her money!

# Stuff I've Learned

Per cent, as I said before, means out of one hundred. Sometimes, you might see it like this – "%".

So this is what I learned – 50% is basically half, so Who Gives A Crap gives away half of all their profits!!!!

If I were to give away 10% of my profits that would be 10 in every 100 so £10 in every £100.

If I make £300, I would give away £10 + £10 + £10 = £30

I have to admit that my mum helped me out on a few of these questions.

# Chapter 3
# Getting Started

Dad had taken the boys out, so me and Mum had some time. I was excited. Mum knows how to make many things but lip balm isn't one of them so we decided to go online and watch YouTube videos about making lip balm together. I typed in "making organic lip balm".

First, we saw a lady in India who was making lip balm for her daughter because she lived far away and she missed her. We didn't actually see her, just her hands stirring the wooden spoon into a pot of lip balm ingredients. As she began explaining how much she missed her daughter, I think she grew sadder and sadder and I thought I might have seen a tear fall into the pot. It was making me feel sad, so I asked Mum if we could watch another one.

Next up was a young lady in America called Shania. Shania had long blonde hair, beautiful teeth and glossy lips. Yes, this definitely was the video to watch. "Hi, guys!" she began excitedly. Unfortunately, after that, she kept swearing so Mum switched that one off pretty quickly.

"Maybe I should check them first before I show you," she said, closing her laptop firmly.

I have to say that I was disappointed as Shania seemed to have really good lips and it would have been great to see what she put on them but I get it, what came out of her mouth wasn't so great.

Mum went on the computer and found some recipes for lip balm and asked me to read them while she went to find more videos. Most of the recipes used coconut butter, beeswax and an oil like almond, avocado or sunflower and then they added some essential oils for the scent – things like peppermint, lavender, vanilla, sweet orange. There were lots of choices. I don't like the smell or taste of peppermint so that was easy; it had to go. Some smells remind me of people – I love lavender! It reminds me of my ammamma and when I used to go to her house, we would collect lavender from her garden. She would dry it and put it in her pillows and when I slept at her house, there was a lovely smell of lavender to fall asleep to. Sadly, she died a year ago. She had an accident. Mum asks me not to share the details of her accident and just tell people that she was run over by a car. She was in fact chasing a cabbage that had rolled out of her bag onto the road and as she went to pick it up, she was hit by a red car.

I sometimes think of it – killed by a cabbage! And I laugh. Ammamma would want me to laugh because she was really funny and accident-prone. Once she superglued her eye shut because she thought the glue was eye ointment. She had to go to the hospital but was laughing about it. Another time, she broke her foot; she was trying to kick the back door open because the painters had painted it shut.

In the beginning, just after she died, I cried a lot and missed her and her funny ways. Like when we used to eat together – we'd have upside-down dinners so we would start with the dessert first and then eat the main meal last. So when my mum asked if she could do anything to make things better, I told her about upside-down dinners but it just wasn't the same. You know when you try to enjoy something but you don't? Then, I asked Mum to buy lavender because we don't have a garden to grow it so she bought the oil. Now, every time the pillows are washed, Mum sprinkles a few drops of lavender on them and this seems to work – I dream of Ammamma and have adventures with her. She would be proud of this lip-balm-making adventure. Yes, definitely, lavender had to be in it because, in some sort of strange way, she would be with me.

My next favourite smell is vanilla – I think vanilla ice cream is probably the best invention in the whole world. When I think of vanilla it just makes me happy. I hoped that vanilla would make other people happy so this could go in it too.

I watched a few more videos with Mum. "So, Anjali, are you ready to pick your ingredients?"

"Coconut butter, beeswax, almond oil, lavender and vanilla," I stated confidently.

And that was it. Mum just said, "Great choice." Which I was pretty surprised about because most times, she ends with, "Are you sure?"

"Come on then, let's go," she said, getting up.

"Where?" I was intrigued because we weren't allowed out anywhere!

"To order the ingredients online."

That's the thing about my mum: once she has an idea in her head, you can't really stop her. The problem is, though, she gets bored pretty quickly (we have a whole cupboard of unfinished arts and crafts) and so we would probably make a batch or two and then stop.

I paused, and then asked, "Mum, do you think we could see this through to the end?"

"What do you mean?"

"Well, you know, we never quite finish things and, well, things always seem to go wrong."

"Anjali," she said, grabbing her purse confidently, "this time, things will be different."

Coins started falling out as she hadn't closed it properly and, well, to be honest with you, I wanted to believe her. We gathered the coins up and went online. Mum was going to lend me £50.

# Stuff I've Learned

Sometimes you have to be careful what you click on while you're on the internet. Lovely lips don't always mean nice things come out of them!

# Chapter 4
# Get Measuring!

There were hundreds of products of everything. ABSOLUTELY EVERYTHING. We looked at our list and typed in "beeswax" first. The "organic beeswax 750 grams" cost double the price of the non-organic one and this was the case for most of the ingredients. Mum asked if I was sure that all the products had to be organic.

For just one moment, I thought we could save a lot of money buying the non-organic products but I started reading all the list of chemicals and I said to myself, *Anjali, you are going to do this properly and it's not about making lots of money, it's about making something natural that you will love and will make others happy.* Well, I'm sure I didn't think exactly this at the time but something like, *Anjali, don't buy chemicals. Don't pollute the earth!* And I was thinking about Mrs Marston and how everything she used had no chemicals. So I told Mum that we were sticking to organic and that I would use the money that Ammamma had given me for my last birthday. (I hadn't spent it because I didn't want to let go of it, but she would be happy for me to spend it on this.)

One by one we bought the ingredients. They were as follows:

French lavender oil 10 ml                    £6.50

Vanilla fragrance oil 10 ml                   £6.99

Vitamin E – 50 ml                             £9.99

Organic coconut oil 500 ml          £6.49
   (I chose this because £2 of it went back
                to the farmers)

Sweet almond oil 100 ml     £12.99
 (it said it was climate-change friendly)

Organic beeswax      £8.98
  (this was on sale. It was £12)

I wasn't even sure how many lip balms that was going to make and we still needed to buy the containers for the lip balms and the packaging. To be honest, right at that moment, I wanted to stop and tell Mum that it was a terrible idea and I wasn't sure how we were going to pull it off... but as I handed over the £50 note that Ammamma had given me, she looked at me in a really proud, tearful way. I could tell she didn't want to take the money.

"Take it, Mum. This is our business."

"Tell you what, Anjali, let me buy you the containers and the packaging." She smiled.

We looked online for small lip balm containers but none of them were right. I wanted something biodegradable (dissolves into the earth and doesn't pollute) but they only seemed to have aluminium containers which Mum convinced me that we could recycle by asking people to just ask for lip balm refills. I agreed and she bought forty small containers, which cost £19.

Mum asked what we had spent.

"£70.94 altogether," I said without hesitating. This was because I saw the total in the online basket!

"Great, Anjali. Do you know how much each lip balm is going to cost us to make?"

I had no idea.

"Well, we have forty tins so if we divide... well, let's round £70.94 to the nearest pound. Actually, let's say we have spent £70. Do you know how much each lip balm tin would have cost us to make?"

I still had no idea and I felt my "fff"s coming.

"Don't worry about it," she said, holding my hand. "There's lots of time to work things out. Shall we move on to the labels?"

Designing things is my absolute favourite thing to do and we went on a site called Zazzle where you can design lots of labels. Mum just left me to it and this is what I came up with:

BUT, Mum pointed out that she thought that the label was way too big for the tin. The labels were 6 cm wide and when we looked at the measurement of the lip balm tin it was 4 cm wide. That could have been a disaster! I needed help but Mum said I could work it out. The next label size was 38 mm. At first, I wasn't sure if they would fit but then I realised that was 3.8 cm, which was less than 4 cm. Yes! I think that was right. Mum nodded. All that was done without any "fff"s in sight!

After I put in 3.8 cm and checked everything, Mum ordered it. It cost the same to order a hundred as it did forty so Mum put in an order of five sheets of twenty, which cost $20. I didn't realise at the time that the labels were American and would be coming from America. Not that I have anything against America but that's being transported on a plane and that's not really environmentally friendly. I thought hard about it and decided this one time would be okay and when Lockdown was over, we could ask the local printer.

Just then my brothers came home and it was chaos. Sons wanted to see what we were doing on the computer so he jumped up and began banging keys on the table. Luckily, we had just finished. Every day, I think, *Today is the day I will not fight with him*. But something always happens.

"Stop that right now, Sons!" I screamed at him.

"Stop that right now, Sons," he mimicked. "Come on, Mendy, say dat." (He can't say his t's.)

"No!" Mendy screamed. Sons used to be able to get Mendy to do anything he wanted but since Lockdown, Mendy doesn't listen to him as much.

"Please stop it. All of you just stop it," Mum bellowed. My mum is normally very calm and patient but since Lockdown, she shouts more. Both the boys started to cry.

"Perhaps you can help Anjali later?" Mum added, trying to calm them down.

They stopped suddenly. That's the thing about them, there is sometimes a lot of fake crying.

Help me? I couldn't let them help, it would be a disaster! As I said, me and Sons don't go five minutes without an argument and Mendy, well, he's only four and he just likes to lick everything. So I said no and they both started to cry again.

I sort of gave in then. "Okay, maybe you can be testers. You can test if the lip balm is good after we've made it."

Mendy smiled and made his "MMMM" sound. He does that a lot when he agrees with something. I'm sure he had no idea what a tester was but I can give him any old job and he's happy – that's what he's like.

"No," Sons shouted. "I want a better dob." (He can say his j's but he's just lazy!)

"Packaging. Helping me wrap up the lip balms to send them out."

He thought about it for a while. "Okay," he replied. He wouldn't last long in packing. Alfonso gets bored after five minutes of anything.

"And you can also be a tester."

"Tank you, Didi," he replied. (That's what he calls me.)

# Stuff I've Learned

It's important to get measurements right. The lip balm label could have looked like one big floppy sun hat on the tin!

It was a good idea to convert mm into cm so everything is the same, which makes it easier to see the difference!

So 3.8 cm is 38 mm as there are 10 mm in each centimetre.

# Chapter 5
# Making Our Lip Balm

Everything arrived by the weekend and on Saturday, Mum was in the kitchen and was very enthusiastic. She had laid out all the ingredients. "Come on then, Anjali, let's do this!"

Due to experience, I had a funny feeling in my stomach that this wasn't going to go well. Mum handed me an apron. "The ingredients we have make up four tins so, we should really start with a small batch," she explained as she glanced at the sheet she had printed off. I nodded. "So let's make forty," Mum announced, looking up.

"Forty? Forty? Forty isn't small. That's ten

times more!"

"That's right, Anjali, we just multiply all the ingredients by ten. So if it says a tablespoon here, we just add ten tablespoons."

"Are you sure, Mum?"

"Yes, let's just go for it!" Mum answered.

I had been here before. For the school fair, she said she would bake twenty cupcakes and then she said she could just add five times the ingredients and make a hundred, so she started randomly throwing in the flour without measuring properly, cracking open boxes of eggs, adding sugar and butter just guesstimating (I'm not sure that's a word but it should be) as she thought it looked roughly the amount she needed. The whole thing was a disaster and the cakes were the only things that did not sell at the fair. In fact, children came back with them asking if they could have their money back. It was so embarrassing.

"Mum, I think we should just stick to what it says and make four."

"Oh, okay, boss," she replied.

"I'll get the measuring jug and

tablespoons," I said. I liked being the boss.

We poured two cups of hot water into a saucepan and put this to boil on a medium flame on the cooker. (Mum helped me with this part.)

Then we put an empty bowl on top of this and a spoon in between the saucepan and the bowl so the steam could come out. Next, we added four tablespoons of coconut oil, four tablespoons of almond oil and then four tablespoons of beeswax until it all melted. We turned the gas off. So far so good, and it only took about five minutes. Next, I added five drops of vitamin E, five drops of vanilla and Mum said she would add the lavender. I'd say that this was the point that it started to go wrong.

The smell of the lavender probably reminded her of Ammamma and maybe she got distracted thinking about her as it wasn't five drops, it was more like ten.

"This reminds me of Ammamma – you know, I started a business with her when I was your age." She smiled.

Don't get me wrong, I was really interested

in what business they had started and to hear what she had done with Ammamma but I was starting to worry about the lip balm. I wanted to say something like perhaps she should stop stirring and pour the mixture into the mixing jug but, just like the Indian woman in the YouTube video, a tear started to form and dropped into the mixture.

"We had a counter in the back of an Indian grocery store and sold dosas together," she reminisced. (A dosa is a South Indian sort of a pancake. I love them and Ammamma used to make them all the time in the way I like them – thin and crispy – and I used to eat about six of them. But Mum's… well, let's just say they turn out like a thick pizza base but I don't say anything and always just stop at one and say I'm not hungry.)

Anyway, how could I stop her from stirring the lip balm mixture? It was going to get cold and would solidify (that means go hard) if she continued talking but then she rarely told me stories about Ammamma; I think it was because it upset her too much.

"We would sell them to lots of customers and sometimes kids from school would walk in and because I was embarrassed, I would hide and disappear behind the counter," she continued.

I do sort of know that feeling. I used to love holding Mum's hand but recently when we go shopping and I bump into someone from school, I drop it quickly.

"Mum," I whispered gently. "The mixture is getting hard and lumpy."

"Oh yes!" Mum looked at the wooden spoon, which had solidified with the beeswax. "We can sort this out no problem." She turned up the heat and the liquid melted again.

"That's science," Mum chuckled and stopped there because Mum doesn't really know too much about science.

The liquid looked like golden honey and smelled DELICIOUS.

Mum poured the mixture into the measuring jug. I laid out the four empty lip balm tins.

"Do you want to pour the liquid in, Anjali?"

It looked tricky but I decided to give it a go. I tried hard to concentrate and not spill any. It was a bit fiddly and I knew I couldn't take too long because the wax would harden. *It will be fine*, I told myself as I held my breath. I filled each container to the top and after I finished, I breathed a huge sigh of relief.

"Well done, Anjali! I think it should take about ten to twenty minutes to solidify," Mum said.

As we tidied up, Mum told me about her many businesses that she had set up as a child. There was a heart-shaped cushion making business (she would make and personalise heart-shaped cushions with people's names) and she thought they would be really popular for Valentine's Day; it didn't take off as Mum didn't like to sew and after the first one Mum got bored. Then there was T-shirt making. She seemed to have some success with this until the red dye that she used to make them washed off and ran into all the other clothes in the washing machine, turning them red. The customers were not happy (neither was Ammamma) and asked for compensation. "Compensation" means not only giving them money back but also money for damaging their other clothes.

I know it was not looking good with her business adventures but when she grew up, she set up a publishing company  because everyone rejected her first book. Mum didn't think that was right so she set up her own company to produce books. She was really successful because she said writing was her true passion and if you are going to set up a business, it's good to do something you love. Also, she says, it's normal to fail a few times but never to give up if it's something you believe strongly in.

The lip balm had solidified and cooled and I called in Sons, our chief tester, and his little assistant, Mendy. We took a pot each. We sniffed it first and it smelled AMAZING – it smelled of lavender and vanilla ice cream. The boys loved the smell. We rubbed a little bit on our fingers. All of us found it slightly difficult to rub and it was a bit lumpy. We dabbed it onto our lips.

Mendy, who is always so easy to please, started to cry. Sons said he had a buzzing feeling on his lips and me, well, for me, it stung, really stung. Mum tried to look calm. "Yes, there is a bit of a stinging feeling there. Come on, children, let's wash our lips." She tried to appear calm as she picked up Mendy and washed his lips. Sons didn't want her to touch his as he liked the feeling but Mum insisted. I washed mine with cold water.

I knew what had happened; she had overdone it with the lavender.

"Mum," I tried not to sound irritated.

"I know, I know, I think I might have gone overboard with the lavender and I think I might have got the amount of coconut oil wrong. Let me see. Yes, I think it should have been one and a half tablespoons, not one."

And instead of saying, I knew it, I knew it would go wrong, like part of me wanted to, I thought she might give up and instead I said, "It's a really good job we only made four. We can do it again later."

Mum smiled and then started to laugh as she picked up Mendy and hugged me and Sons. "Well, I suppose it's a good thing that happened because we have to think of people who have allergies and so we need to label the tins with all the ingredients."

"Don't change anyting about it, Didi. I loved it!"

I knew Sons would be an unreliable tester!

# Stuff I've Learned

The proper amount of ingredients, if any of you want to make my lip balm, are (this makes four small tins):

Coconut oil – one and a half tablespoons of coconut oil (Mum forgot to read the half bit)

Almond oil – one tablespoon

Beeswax – one tablespoon

Vitamin E – five drops

Vanilla oil – five drops

Lavender oil – just a few drops! Perhaps three to five!

AND, most importantly –
one adult to make sure you don't burn yourself.

# Chapter 6
# Going Big!

"I've got one big surprise for you!" Mum was excited as I walked into her bedroom. "I know you weren't very happy about the tins so I went online and ordered a hundred biodegradable pots. They are made with cardboard and lined with wax so you can pour liquid into them."

I looked at the images on the laptop. They looked great. I saw the price: $65 including shipping. DOLLARS? DOLLARS? So they would have to be flown on a plane to get here – what about air pollution? I tried not to look disappointed.

"Have you already bought them, Mum?"

"Yes, I wanted to surprise you!"

How could I break it to her? A few months ago, I think I would have just screamed, "Are you serious, Mum? Really? Think of the sky you are polluting, the birds you are killing, the air you are contaminating." But I have learned that doesn't really work with Mum. When I scream, she says, "No television time," very calmly. This makes me even madder and sometimes, I will respond with, "I don't care," to which she will say, "Don't speak to me like that – go to your room."

If I slam the door shut, which sometimes I do, she will come after me and say, "A week of no television." I haven't tested her on what will happen if I say, "I don't care." Because I do care and I don't want her to take the television away permanently or sell it.

I took a deep breath and calmly told her what I thought.

A look of panic came over her face.

"Oh no. I wasn't thinking!"

"And it says here that it will take three weeks. That's a long time to wait."

"I'm sorry, Anjali. I thought they would

47

be perfect."

"Mum, I am really grateful," I said (because I was to have a mum who likes to surprise me), "but next time, can we make all the decisions together?"

"Yep, definitely, two heads are better than one," she replied.

"Shall we get started?" I asked.

She closed her laptop and we went into the kitchen.

The recipe we had made four lip balms – we had to make ten times that. This was going to be tricky!

"Do we just multiply everything by ten, Mum?"

"Yes, and I think I'll let you measure everything out. You seem to be more precise."

One by one, she handed me the ingredients and I measured out the coconut oil and the beeswax carefully with the tablespoon and heated them together in a pan. Then I added the almond oil and switched the gas off. I took the vitamin E, added the drops and then the vanilla drops and as I reached for the lavender, I said to Mum, "We can't cry – let's put happy thoughts into this because Ammamma would be really happy that we are doing this." Mum nodded and smiled as I opened the lavender and put in just ten drops and as I did this, I thought of Ammamma laughing her head off at her own clumsiness. I thought of her hanging out her freshly washed laundry ready to put lavender in the pillows so we would fall asleep soundly. I thought of us gardening together and this warm glow came over me and it was love and I knew that my recipe was made with love. I looked at the golden liquid and felt proud.

Because we had made a big batch, it was difficult to pour into the jug so Mum did this bit and then it had to go into the little tins. This was complicated as the mixture was very hot and the jug was heavy, so Mum said she would do this too. I was nervous for her. When I did this the first time, I held my breath for nearly a minute. We were making ten times the amount so if she held her breath for ten minutes, she would probably pass out or die. My "fff"s were about to come out so I just said, "I'm scared, Mum."

"Don't worry, Anjali, what could go wrong?"

*Erm, well, a lot!* I thought. *She could pass out or die, she could burn herself, the liquid could go everywhere, the wax might not come off...*

"It will be okay and if I make a mess of it, no big deal."

"Okay, but don't hold your breath when you pour it in," I replied anxiously.

Mum's hand wobbled as she poured the first tin. It overflowed and the liquid went everywhere.

"Don't worry, Anjali, I'll get the hang of this."

I wanted to cry as I found it nail-biting to watch. The next one she didn't fill up as much. I'd say by the time she got to the tenth one, she had done it – perfectly! But then the wax had solidified and it became harder to pour.

"Don't worry, Anjali." She boiled up the pan again and put the jug into the boiling water. To my relief, the mixture melted back into liquid.

"Science." Mum smiled as she continued and by the time she got to the end, I was really proud of her. Yes, there was a big mess of wax on the table but she had done it and they weren't perfect but that was okay.

"They look amazing, Mum!"

"These ones here don't look full – shall I just refill them?" she asked.

Before I knew it, she was refilling the half-empty ones but because they had already begun to solidify, the wax she put on top looked uneven and lumpy.

"Maybe not," she decided after doing a couple.

And there they were, our first forty lip balms made! We left them to set as we washed up.

"Mum," I said, handing her the empty jug, "I think this is one of the best things we have ever done together."

"Me too," she replied.

❀ ❀ ❀

The lip balms had set and they looked like

perfect little puddles of wax that you would never want to jump into and they smelled of vanilla ice cream with lavender. Okay, there might have been one or two that were imperfect with blobs of wax on them but it didn't matter. I felt proud of Mum and myself – we had done it!

"Time to test," Mum called out to the boys.

Before you knew it, they came crashing into the kitchen ready to do their jobs.

"Let me go first, just in case," Mum insisted.

She took one of the imperfect lip balms, held out her index finger and let it glide around the surface of the lip balm like a professional ice skater and then she applied it to her lips. I waited with my breath held as she pursed them together and smiled.

"Feels great, it's smooth and, wait... no tingling, it's safe to try."

Alfonso was the first to dig in – literally. He managed to scoop out a blob of wax with his fingers and pasted it to his lips. "Yum!" He licked his lips.

"You're not meant to eat it, Sons," I told him.

"I'm not!" he shouted at me.

"Come here, Mendy, let me put it on for you." Mendy always lets me try things on him. Once, after watching *Horrible Histories*, I gave him a full fashion makeover complete with Mum's high heels and turned him into Queen Elizabeth (the one with the red hair).

"Smells nice, Didi." He smiled.

Then, excitedly, I applied some to my lips. Okay, so I have tried a lot of lip balms because of the "fff" situation and this one was like ice cream on the lips: soothing, cooling and that smell. It was AMAZING!

"We did it, Mum, we really did it!"

"We certainly did, Juju B." (That is a name she calls me when she is especially happy or when she wants me to feel things are not so bad.)

"Yes, I did it too!" Sons joined in. Normally an argument would start as I would say he had nothing much to do with it and then he would call me something and then there would be a fight. But I felt happy and I wanted to stay happy so I said, "Thank you for your help, Sons, and yours too, Mendy."

Sons dug his finger back into the lip balm

and took out another clump. I think Mum must have been tired because she didn't say anything. "Let's put the lids on them and pack them away." Mum hurried us along.

The boys helped us and we put them back into the cardboard box that the tins had come in. We kept the four wonky ones (the testers) aside and wrote our names on the tins.

"I think I'll keep a hold of yours, boys," Mum insisted. Sons was about to protest when Mum distracted him with an offer of a snack – he is easily distracted like that. You don't have to distract Mendy with anything; he's much better behaved. Mum said they could eat it in the living room. We can only eat food in the living room for special occasions.

"We're gonna sell these to our friends and family, right, Mum?"

"Going to," she corrected me. "Well, yes, minus the four."

And without thinking, I asked how much we would make from thirty-six lip balms and then I realised it was a maths problem.

Normally, my "fff"s would start bobbing to the surface so I don't know if it was the lip balms or the excitement of having made them but I felt nothing.

"We have to do some research first, Anjali. We need to see what similar lip balms cost. That's seeing what the competition is doing."

"Competition? What competition? Who entered a competition?" I asked.

"The competition or competitors are people who make similar products to you. Come here, I'll show you."

She typed in "homemade organic lip balm" on her phone and clicked "shop" on Google. A whole lot of lip balms came up. "See here."

There were lip balms for £10 and over! Then Mrs Marston's Magic Lip Balm came up. There she was – Mrs Marston (still no face, just her products). I wondered if she had received my letter. Mrs

*Mrs Marston's Magical Lip balm*

Marston's was £8 and then there were some balms that looked like ours that cost £4 and £5.

"I think we should start at £3 because we've just begun and we don't really know what we're doing," I suggested.

"Good idea," Mum agreed.

So that was £3 multiplied by thirty-six. I took out a sheet of paper to do the maths on. £108.

"Is that £108, Mum?"

"Hang on a minute." She took out her phone. This is the part I don't get. WHY ARE ADULTS ALLOWED TO USE THEIR CALCULATORS?

"That's right, Anjali... that's right!" The second "that's right" was one that was not trying to sound too excited but I knew she was.

"£108 is called "turnover". Turnover is what we will make if we sell all thirty-six lip balms, but we have to take away expenses."

Now it was getting complicated.

"Do you know what expenses are?"

Mum asked.

I could feel the "fff"s starting.

"Oh, it's just the things that you've spent money on like the ingredients you used to make the lip balm and the tins." Mum tried not to make a big deal out of it. "Can you remember how much that was?"

"Around £70?"

"Yes, and don't forget to add, say, £15 for the labels, so that's..."

"£85," I answered without thinking.

"Great, so you have to take away £85 from £108 and this is the profit that you made. The money you get to keep. Do you understand?"

She'd lost me at £85 so she sat me down and explained again.

Basically, if you make something and you want to sell it, you have to take away how much it cost you to make. I got it and there were no "fff"s or feelings of panic. So our profit would be £23.

"Then you want to give 10 per cent to charity, but we will come back to that one later," Mum said quickly. "I think that's more than enough for now."

I wanted to stop with the maths, but I wanted to continue with making the lip balms. "When will we sell them? We can start selling them to the family. We can start that now."

"The only thing I'm starting now is dinner. Otherwise, we will have two hungry monsters and you know what happens to them when they get hungry."

Sons gets hangry, like a ravenous beast – he rampages through the house causing mischief. Once he sprayed shaving cream all over the bathroom trying to write the word "hungry" but he can't spell very well and we weren't sure what it said. Mendy just gets quiet and says "Hmmm" quite a lot.

"Can I do it, Mum, please? Can I ring around, first just the relatives? Please? Can I borrow your phone?" I pleaded. Lots of kids in my class have their own phones. My friends are allowed to call me but on my mum's phone and sometimes this is sooo embarrassing. Sometimes, Mum will have chats with them and she reads ALL the text messages, ALL of them, and if I try deleting them, I'm in trouble.

She handed me her phone and I was shocked.

"But what do I say?"

"Just tell them what you're doing and ask if they would like to help you by buying a lip balm."

My first call was to Grandad. Grandad is easy, firstly because he doesn't really listen and all I have to say is "£3" and he will say, "For you, make it £10," which is exactly what he did. Which made my next call feel easier. I called my uncle, and he is an entrepreneur with lots of wild ideas. He is currently working on supplying electric batteries to people – I'm not sure what for, but he says that this is an eco-friendly option. He has done lots of things. Mum said that when he was little, he used to get up to all sorts of mischief and Sons reminds her of him. He once found a bike, painted it different colours and sold it but it turned out that the bike belonged to someone and he got into a lot of trouble for that.

"Brilliant idea," he said. "I'll take ten."

Ten! Ten!! That was £30. Was this maths getting easier?

That left twenty-five lip balms to sell because Grandad insisted on buying one for £10.

The next call was to my godmother, Avni. She is an accountant and when I told her why we started the business she was very impressed and bought eight. That was, until I told her my uncle had bought ten. "I'll take twelve, then," she insisted.

Twelve! Twelve!! There were only thirteen lip balms left and I still had a long list of people to get through. The rest got sold in two phone calls: one to my aunt, who doesn't buy anything unless it's organic, and the rest went to my mum's friend Monica, who called while I was speaking to my aunt. I told her what I was doing and that was that.

I handed the phone back to my mum.

"All sold," I replied.

"No way!"

"Yes!" I smiled proudly.

Sons was figuring out what he could spend the money on. I knew what I wanted to do. I wanted to put the money back into the business and make more lip balms – we still had ingredients left and the cases were coming all the way from America. "Can we build a website, Mum?" I asked. If I had a website, I would call it Anjali's Organics.

"No." She shook her head. When she does this, I know that it is a definite no but I always try to change her mind.

"Please?"

"No."

"I'll give you three good reasons why a website is a good idea." She is always telling me to convince her instead of just pleading.

"One: because to have a website is important if we are serious. Two: people can order and pay online. Three—" I didn't get to three because she said "NO" firmly.

"What about if I made £300? That's enough for a website, isn't it?"

"If you make £300, Anjali, you can have a website." She laughed. Her laugh was a bit like a cackle – not like a witch's cackle, but it was a laugh that said she didn't think I could do it.

"Pinky promise, Mum?"

"Yes, Anjali. I pinky promise."

"Can I eat in ten minutes? It's just that I have something I quickly need to do."

She nodded.

All day, I'd wanted to find out more about Mrs Marston so just before dinner, I went on the internet to see what else I could find out about her.

There was a blank space where her profile picture was. I don't think it was because she was afraid of internet security, because according to her biography she had been an intrepid adventurer who travelled the world in her biplane. She was almost eaten by a tiger – yes, a tiger when her biplane crashed in the jungles of Borneo. Alone and frightened, Louisa (that was her first name) was about to die of starvation. She was

writing her final goodbyes in a letter to her parents when a tribesman found her and carried her back to the tribe.

I read on, intrigued.

The tribe didn't have a doctor as we know them but used plants for healing. He used plant teas and ointments to treat her wounds. Mrs Marston was well enough to leave after a few months but she decided to stay with the tribe for six months; she wanted to learn more about the healing properties of plants and how the tribespeople could heal themselves of illnesses. If the truth be told, after six more months she didn't want to leave the tribe, but she believed she had a message to spread to the world about the magical nature of plants, caring for the environment and not polluting with chemicals.

So when she arrived back home in England, she began making creams from the oils from the plants which she gathered in forests. At first, nobody wanted to buy them as they thought it was all nonsense but slowly, her business began to grow and she got a business partner (someone who would help her grow her business). The business made lots of money but then one day, the business partner ran off with all the profits leaving Mrs Marston heartbroken.

I imagined her staying in bed for weeks and weeks, not wanting to get up. This is what I wanted to do when Ammamma died but I didn't want to let Mum know how heartbroken I was because I think she wanted to do the same. Then Mrs Marston read an article about deforestation (cutting down of beautiful forests) in the Amazon Rainforest and I imagined her leaping out of bed to protest. I am not sure if she made a placard and protested but what she did do was buy a plane ticket and went to South America to learn more about the forest and its plants. Once again she spent time with the tribes and brought back more knowledge and started again, and this time she called her business Mrs Marston's Magical Creams and she had no business partners.

Mrs Marston became a millionaire and

then the coolest thing of all happened – she gave most of her money away to charities that helped the environment. That was where the story ended. I wondered what had happened to her and her secret ingredients and if she was still alive and if she would respond to my letter because I was desperate to meet her.

# Stuff I've Learned

Turnover – this might sound like a nice apple pie but it is the amount a business takes. Say I take £300 a year. This is my turnover. Profit. If I take £300 and I have spent £120 on all the ingredients, I have £180 left – this is the profit I made. The £120 I spent on stuff like oils and wax are called EXPENSES. Complicated, I know! It took me ages to understand!

# Chapter 7
# Nature Is Amazing!

"Kids, dinner time," Mum called out.

I have a strong sense of smell and from my bedroom, I could smell it was dosa or pizza base! My heart sank just a little bit because I just wanted to taste Ammamma's dosas again – thin, crispy and buttery.

"Surprise! I've made your favourite," she said, handing me two dosas. I tried to look happy. I know I should tell her that they are not my favourite thing to eat any more but I don't want to upset her.

Over dinner, I told Mum and Dad about the amazing Mrs Marston but it was chaotic as it always is with Sons throwing his food everywhere and interrupting every five minutes. Dad seemed to know stuff about plant medicine and he said he had a book somewhere that he would give me. I looked at the dehydrated mint plant sitting at the kitchen counter in a whole new light. I had never really seen it before – what did mint do?

After dinner, I gave the mint plant a little drink of water.

"Thank you, Anjali, I've been meaning to do that all day," Mum commented.

Sons got up to give it another drink.

"Don't do that," I said. "It's had enough. Go and water another plant."

But he wanted to water THAT one and so began fighting with me AGAIN! This time, I walked away and I could hear him pretending to howl as Mum pulled him away from the plant.

Sometimes, I have to admit, I love bedtimes because it's just my time. The boys share a room and so I have my own room and they are absolutely not allowed to come in without my permission.

In my room, I have this massive desk bed which is way too big for the room. It has a desk and sofa on the bottom and a bunk bed on top and even though it is way too big, I love it because it's my space. I was sitting on the sofa part when Dad knocked. I can

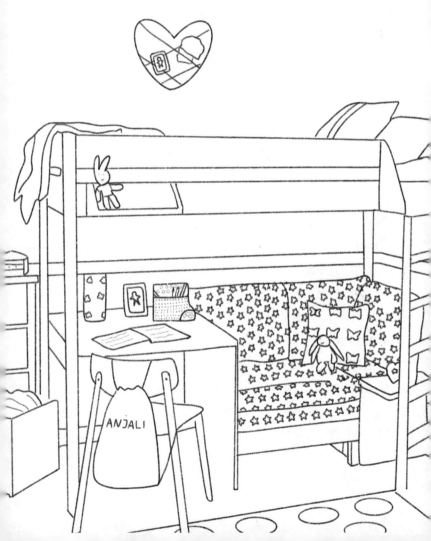

tell his knock from anywhere because he always knocks with some rhythm. He came in with the book that he was telling me about, *Healing Plants & Herbs*, and OMG, do you know who it was written by? The one and only Mrs Marston! I couldn't believe it! I was desperate to see a photograph of her and grabbed the book and opened it but there was none.

"Dad, it's Mrs Marston. Mrs Marston is the author – you know, the lady I was telling you about?"

Dad sat beside me. I didn't know where to start and began flicking through the pages – I was beyond HAPPY!

Dad is very busy with work but he will always sit with me at bedtime and we will talk about different things. My dad loves meditation, nature and is a great dancer. I don't really talk to him about meditation but we always have lots to talk about when it comes to nature and when we used to go out to parties, he and I would always be the first to dance!

Sometimes, Dad and I don't talk about

anything and he just sits with me and reads a book.

"Shall we start with mint?" I asked because I was thinking about the dehydrated mint plant that Sons wanted to drown in water.

He turned to the page that said "*Mentha*" (he told me that this is mint's scientific name).

Apparently, the Greeks put it on their arms thinking that it would make them stronger and it is used to treat stomach aches. Maybe Mum knows this? She always drinks her mint tea when she feels she has eaten too much chocolate. Did I tell you my mum is a chocoholic? (Someone who LOVES chocolate and eats it all the time.) Once I got a chocolate Easter bunny and I left it in the cupboard, telling her NOT to eat it. She secretly ate the ears and when I checked on it, it had turned into a gerbil.

I couldn't believe it until I found out that was actually a replacement bunny/gerbil. She had eaten the original one and asked Dad to go to the shop to get another one to replace it (this was before Lockdown).

I actually laughed when I found this part out. I'm not really into chocolate so it didn't bother me that much and secretly, I like it that Mum is a rulebreaker.

As we were finished reading about mint, I suddenly thought about the ingredients for our lip balm. "Lavender, is lavender in here, Dad?"

"*Lavandula*," he said, turning to the page.

The Greeks used it 2,500 years ago to help them get to sleep and they put it on their body to help them get rid of aches and pains. They seemed to put everything on their body!

The Romans then put it in soaps and the Victorians used it as a disinfectant and until World War One, lavender was used to treat wounds like an antiseptic and did you know that for hundreds of years, English farmers would put lavender in their hats to stop them from getting headaches?

I wanted to discover what vanilla did but was too tired.

"Goodnight."

"Goodnight, Anjali."

"It's really cool, isn't it, Dad?"

"What?"

"It's so cool that nature gives us all these herbs and plants."

"It really is," he replied.

I went to sleep on my pillow that smelled of lavender and had a dream that I was lost in the jungles of Borneo and was rescued by a tribesman who handed me all his secret recipes in a language I didn't understand. "These will be given to you," he said. "Make sure you take care of them."

# Stuff I've Learned

I think plants have feelings. We did an
experiment – we bought two identical plants
and named them Maggie and Michael. To Maggie,
we said really lovely things like "I love you!
You are very beautiful..." and we touched
her a lot. We ignored Michael. Sons wanted
to call Michael names but Mum put her foot
down and said no and we didn't put much love
into it when we watered it (this was part of
the experiment – not to talk to him). Maggie
shot up very quickly and looked very healthy.
Michael, unfortunately, didn't grow very much
and looked as if it had battled a storm.
Okay, so maybe I can't prove that they have
feelings but I know that they respond to love.
So, now I have to tell you what we did to
Michael. We flooded him with love. Every day,
we sang to him (well, I asked Sons not to

because he screeches) but we told him how great he looked and how important he was and we let Mendy stroke him gently. Do you know, he got better and grew to be the same size as Maggie.

# Chapter 8
# Zoom & Gloom

Okay, I had to wait a bit for my cardboard packaging to arrive from America and in the meantime, I had to get on with my schoolwork. At the beginning of Lockdown, there was no online learning for us. The teachers just used to set us work on the school website and we didn't even have to hand it in. Mum sort of checked what we did but not really as she was too busy most of the time trying to stop Sons and Mendy fighting and trying to do her own work and also feed us. I don't know why but Lockdown made us really hungry and every five minutes, one of us seemed to need a snack.

I really missed Leyla and, in the beginning, Mum would hand me her phone so I could WhatsApp her but there was nothing really to talk about. I mean, I told her about making lip balm but it was weird and we would run out of things to say and we NEVER run out of things to say and then Leyla sent me a message saying that she was still my BFF but was finding it really difficult to talk on the phone. I knew that because a lot of the time, she looked as if she wanted to cry so I said, "Let's write letters like in the olden days." So like in the olden days, we started writing letters to each other and posting them through each other's letter boxes (we don't live very far from each other), then I found we had loads to say and it was exciting getting a letter from her and writing one back.

She had started baking in Lockdown and wrote about the cakes she was making and they sounded amazing. Sometimes she would add a drawing. I would tell her about new plants I had discovered, like aloe vera.

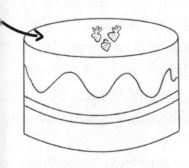

Leyla's cake

Do you know that the aloe vera plant heals burns and generally helps the skin? You can make a paste with the leaves of the plant and put it on a scar on your skin. I haven't done this yet but maybe when Lockdown is over, I will get an aloe vera plant.

Anyway, as the weeks went by our teachers thought it was a good idea to have an online video session. At first, it was hilarious because all you could hear were kids talking and screaming because we were all excited to see each other and each other's houses and our head, Mr D'Souza, just kept shouting, "Mute your mike, mute your mike." At first, no one knew what that was and then the school sent an email to explain what to do. It didn't really seem to help as everyone was just excited to see each other so the school did the video thing once a week but now they asked us to hand work in. It's not that I don't like schoolwork but I didn't want to watch another video of some random stranger from BBC Bitesize explaining something and I wished for a familiar face and then I wished that I hadn't wished for that because instead of Mr D'Souza doing our weekly calls it was, wait for it, Mr Shutgun!

I literally froze when I saw him on screen and then when he asked me a question, I didn't really want to speak to him and I could feel the "fff"s coming out and I know it was wrong but I pretended to freeze. Well, I pretended that the screen had frozen – that was, until Sons and Mendy burst into the room in their underpants and asked what I was doing. I panicked and didn't know what to do so I shut the computer and began to cry.

"Can you not give me just five minutes on my own?" I shouted at the boys.

Mum called out for them and then I felt bad.

In my next letter to Leyla, I told her what I had done and she said she would have done exactly the same and nobody really noticed because Abdul's mum didn't realise that he was online and she appeared on screen waving a pair of his underpants and was telling him off for leaving his underpants on the bathroom floor AGAIN and everyone was laughing. Abdul is very forgetful – you have to tell him things ten times before he remembers anything. Once we were doing a science project together and he was supposed to bring all the stuff in to make the planets and he promised he wouldn't forget, he even wrote the list on his hand and the next day, did he remember? NO! So I get Abdul's mum, I would be screaming at him too. I did feel bad for him, though, as that must have been really embarrassing and he is forever going to be known as "Underpants Abdul" because that's what happens at school!

We didn't have to join the weekly videos and to be honest, they were all a bit strange and left me feeling school-sick (I mean it made me miss school even more). Also, I didn't really want to see Mr Shutgun. Leyla had written that he would be doing them as

Miss Hawthorne was taking some time off. I asked Mum if I really had to join (I didn't tell her about the Mr Shutgun bit) but said they made me miss school even more (which was sort of true). Mum said that it was up to me and it was important to do things that made me happy so there were no more video calls, but I did hand in the work that I was supposed to and counted the days until the lip balm containers would arrive.

# Stuff I've Learned

If you are on a video call and not the speaker, always put yourself on mute. This is what Mr D'Souza meant. And make sure to tell ALL your family that you are going on a call because:
1) You don't want your brothers storming in dressed only in their underpants and
2) You certainly don't want your mum to wave your underpants in front of the camera!

# Chapter 9
# A Disaster!

The labels arrived and then the cardboard packaging arrived from America so Mum and I set to work. We decided to make a batch of ten to test first. Of course, Sons came into the kitchen and wanted to help. I knew that if I gave him a task, he would do it, get bored and then leave so I asked him to lay out the cardboard lip balm containers. All he had to do was to separate the lids and put the cardboard bases on the kitchen table. He laid out about fifty and then, as I said, he got bored and left.

Mum and I concentrated hard and this time we didn't chat. We made the first batch of ten and I carefully poured the liquid gold into the containers. We waited until they had cooled and then we tested a pot... PERFECT. They smelled delicious and not only that, they glided smoothly on the lips and there was no tingling. Mum and I high-fived each other as we continued making two more batches of twenty. We set those lip balms to cool too. They looked magnificent lying there on the kitchen table like mini puddles of honey. As they were setting, Mum began cleaning and I stuck the labels on the lids and I can't tell you how proud I felt. We did it! We really did it!

Once the lip balms had cooled and solidified, we decided that we could put the lids on the cardboard pots. I was so incredibly excited. For some reason, I couldn't put the first lid on so I tried the next pot and the next and weirdly, none of them seemed to fit. I felt really sick – something had gone horribly wrong and I didn't know what it was.

"Mum, something's not right – can you put these lids on?"

Mum tried but she couldn't get the lids on either; they seemed too small. She tried another one and then this worried look came over her face.

"What is it, Mum? ... Mum?"

"The lids aren't the lids. This is the base of the container. See here..."

I didn't understand. "What does that mean?" I panicked.

"Well, I think Alfonso accidentally thought that the lids were the bases – he has muddled them up so the proper lids don't fit any more."

I wanted to cry. "What are we going to do? If they don't fit, that's fifty lip balms wasted."

Right at that minute Sons walked in wanting to test or do another job and right at that minute, if I am being honest, I just wanted to hit him.

"NO, Sons. You have done enough. I knew I shouldn't have let you do this. Whatever you do, IT GOES WRONG!" I screamed at him. Mum kept telling me to stop and Sons started to cry.

"Listen to me, Anjali. It wasn't his fault.

It was an easy mistake to make," she tried calming me.

"Of course it was his fault. Whose else was it?"

Sons was howling and it wasn't his fake howl.

"We should have checked, Anjali. I should have checked."

I knew that I should have checked it too but I was angry.

"It's all your fault, Sons – I knew I shouldn't have given you a job!"

He cried even more.

"Anjali!" Mum picked him up. "Mistakes happen but the most important thing is to learn from them. Look on the bright side, at least we will have lip balms to last us the next ten years."

I didn't find it funny. All the waste, the waste of ingredients, of packaging, labels – what was that going to do to the environment? And – the waste of money. All the profit that I had made was gone and, well, I just wanted to ditch the business. All my hard work for nothing!

Mum said that we could wrap a few of them up in cling film and give them out as gifts to friends and relatives explaining what had happened.

"Cling film? Cling film? Cling film is just more plastic and waste," I replied.

"I know, Anjali, but that's better than throwing them away. Sometimes you have to make the best of a not-great situation."

A not-great situation! It was a disaster!!

"Mum. I'm really sorry but I don't want to do this any more."

"Don't give up, Anjali, you have to see things through."

"But you don't." And as soon as I said it, I regretted it. The words just flew out of my mouth like arrows and I knew one had landed on Mum.

There were two ways this could go – she would either shout at me and tell me off or she would say nothing (which would be worse). She looked at me and said nothing.

I felt awful and left the kitchen, went to my bedroom and burst into tears. I wished we had never started this. Where did it leave me? Me shouting at Sons, Mum being upset with me, wasted lip balms and the money Ammamma had given me had all gone. I crawled under my duvet and just wanted to disappear. Instead, I must have fallen asleep. I dreamed of Mrs Marston in her biplane. She was by herself, happily singing one minute and in the next, her plane crashed and it looked like she wouldn't make it. Days passed, she was hungry and injured and just as she thought she was about to die, she was rescued by a man. It was the same man I had seen in my other dream. I woke up. What did it mean?

I think it meant that if Mrs Marston could be brave, travel across the world and survive a plane crash then I could travel across the sitting room and into the kitchen and say that I was sorry. I jumped out of bed. There was no one in the kitchen. The lip balms were still neatly laid on the table. I took out the cling film from the drawer and cut it into small pieces and began covering the lip balm as best as I could.

Sons burst in. "Do you want to help me, Sons?"

"What are you doing?" he asked. That's the best thing about him. He forgets our arguments really quickly.

"Making lids," I replied.

He sat next to me; the cling film kept getting stuck between his fingers and curling up but it didn't matter.

"I'm sorry for what I said to you, Sons."

"It's okay, Didi," he replied, smiling as he covered his fingers with cling film.

After the lip balms had all been covered, I went to find Mum. She was in the bathroom unloading the washing machine.

"Mum, I'm really sorry about what I said to you."

She looked at me.

"Really, I am."

"No, it's true, Anjali. I don't often finish what I start, especially when things go wrong and that's something I'm going to work on."

I wasn't sure what to say, so I asked her if she needed help with hanging out the washing. She said she did and as we hung out the washing together she told me she had some good news.

"You're going back to school again." She smiled.

We had been at home for six months and at the start, every day before I went to sleep, I wished that this would end and we could go back to school so when she told me, I thought I would be jumping around the house with joy but I wasn't because I was going to miss this time with my family. When we finished, I followed her into the kitchen. A massive smile came over her face when she saw that the lip balms had been covered.

We carefully placed them into a box and Mum said she would deliver them to all the friends and relatives that lived locally and then she said, "Anjali, if you want to, we can stop now. You have learned so much from this."

"Let's see what happens, Mum. I don't think this is the end yet."

# Stuff I've Learned

Having someone accept your apology and forgive you is one of THE BEST feelings EVER!

# Chapter 10
# Hercules And The
# Twelve Labours

After nearly six months off, I was so excited to go back to school and see my friends and also do my show-and-tell about the lip balm business. I walked to school on my own, holding my lip balm proudly in my pocket and a memory stick with my presentation and then as I entered the school gates, I saw some of the children from my class. There was Coco, Krishna and then my BFF, Leyla, and although technically we weren't allowed to hug each other, we couldn't help it. Leyla and I ran into each other's arms and jumped up and down with joy. The bell rang and I couldn't wait to see Miss Hawthorne.

We all went into class, chatting non-stop – BUT WAIT, what was this? Mr D'Souza was in our classroom announcing that Miss Hawthorne was taking some more time off? What? "And so let me introduce you to..."

NO, NO, NO, it wasn't true... Mr, Mr, Mr... Shutgun. He still had the twirly circus moustache but no beard.

"I'm sure most of you already know Mr Shutgun," Mr D'Souza continued.

I could feel the class trying not to groan.

It was like one ginormous burp being kept in. I had my head in my hands. Leyla looked worried. Simon Peters, the class clown, just had a big frown on his face.

"Good morning, 5H," Mr Shutgun said cheerfully. He was probably only doing that because Mr D'Souza was still there and the moment he left, he would probably give out detention to anyone who dropped their pencil.

"Well, Mr Shutgun, I'll leave you to it." Mr D'Souza left the classroom.

"First things first," he said, "let me get to know you. Why don't you write down your name on the piece of paper in front of you, fold it so I can read your name."

Normally, there would be hundreds of questions like, "Can we colour it in? What size should it be?" But no, there were no questions, no chatter. We just got on with it.

"So, did anyone do anything interesting during Lockdown?" Mr Shutgun asked.

I wanted to tell my class about my lip balm business and all the things that went wrong but I looked at Mr Shutgun and I didn't want him to say that it was a stupid thing to do, so I said nothing.

I'm sure lots of the kids in my class did lots of interesting things. Krishna is into the universe big time; he probably built lots of different space models. Coco – she's really good with her imagination and draws all kinds of mythical creatures, and then there's Fatima, who probably came up with a whole load of new jokes to try on us... But no, nobody said a word, not even Mark Chomsky, who ALWAYS has something to say and our class didn't seem like our class without the chatter. It was like a big dark cloud came and sat above our classroom.

"Well," Mr Shutgun continued, "I'm sure we will hear your stories as the day progresses."

Shilpa put her hand up. I thought she had cracked as she likes to show off her new Bollywood dance routines on ANY occasion. Sad moment – doesn't matter, her Bollywood dance comes out. Someone getting shouted at, Bollywood dance comes out. "Sir, no offence, but when is Miss

Hawthorne coming back?" Shilpa asked.

Some of us gasped because this was the question we all wanted to ask.

I wanted to cover my eyes. Even though I'm not friends with Shilpa and I think she can be bossy, I didn't want her to get told off.

"That's a good question." Mr Shutgun looked down at the name that she had written. She didn't even bother placing her musical notes around it – that's what she normally does. "I'm not sure, Shilpa."

There was no follow-up joke from Simon Peters as there normally would be. "Any other questions before we begin?" Mr Shutgun asked.

There were none.

I thought we were going to get straight into maths. That's what normally happens on a Monday but Mr Shutgun decided to play a quiz with us. He gave each table a name (we were called Rugby – I'm not sure why) and he started asking us all kinds of general knowledge questions like: what is the planet closest to the sun? How many sides does a decagon have? Who was the lady in Greek mythology with the snake hair? At first, it was very quiet but by the end of the game, we were lively and he didn't tell us off so we continued and it felt kind of normal again. Krishna's table won as I knew they would – there isn't anything that he doesn't know and they got ten house points.

Fatima put up her hand. "Sir, over the holidays. I came up with a few new jokes."

"We would love to hear them..." (he looked at her name) "... Fatima. Come to the front of the class."

Wait, was this the same Mr Shutgun? Same circus moustache but no beard. Did he have a kinder twin brother?

I was scared for Fatima. What if he said her jokes were rubbish?

Fatima went up excitedly and began.

"Why did the chicken cross the road?"

Simon Peters shouted out, "Why?"

"Because the chicken next to it didn't know how to socially distance properly!"

We started to laugh. Fatima continued.

"Did you hear the one about the virus

joke? ... Never mind, I don't want to spread it around!"

We laughed and some of us groaned and I'd say it felt as if we had gone back to normal. One by one the kids started putting up their hands to share what they had done during Lockdown.

"Okay, this is how we'll do it: we will hear from a few of you throughout the day so after maths, let's hear from Coco and Simon," Mr Shutgun stated.

And there it was, the dreaded M-word – maths. I was sure that he would show his true dark side then.

"5H. Today we are doing a test. It's just to see where you are all at and there is absolutely no need to panic or be afraid." Leyla, my BFF, looked at me and then looked afraid. "If you don't know a question, just move on to the next one."

Normally, it would be at this point that my "fff"s would come out but surprisingly nothing happened. Perhaps it was because I was too focused on when Mr Shutgun's cover would be blown. He handed out the maths questions and said we had half an hour to complete it.

The first few questions were easy and then it got harder and by the end, it was all about percentages, fractions and multiplying decimals but I managed to finish and check my work and I sat there.

He came over to me.

"Anything wrong?" He looked at my name. "Anjali."

"No, I've finished," I replied.

He looked at his watch.

"Twenty minutes. Are you sure?"

I nodded.

"Okay, well. Double-check it, please."

So I checked it again and I sat there.

"Okay, class. Time is up."

Then the bell for break time went.

At break time, I showed Leyla my lip balm; she smelled it and said it reminded her of vanilla ice cream on a sunny day and that I should share the story of making the lip balm with the class. I didn't bring Leyla a lip balm because she would worry about the ingredients. As I told you before, Leyla worries about absolutely everything. And then she said something mysterious had happened to the worry cloud that followed her around, which changed everything.

"So, I met the Secret Baker," she whispered.

The Secret Baker is someone who lives on the hill and makes cakes. (You can decide how much you want to pay for the cake and all the money goes to charity.) Nobody knows who the Secret Baker is.

"No way!" I screamed.

I didn't get a chance to ask her how or what had happened because the bell went. Playtime seemed to end very quickly.

We learned about Greek mythology and the Twelve Labours of Hercules. He seemed to have an awful lot of obstacles: to fight the lion, to kill the Hydra, to capture a belt... which made my obstacles making lip balm feel not so big! And it seemed a lot of things to do for forgiveness.

Mr Shutgun was firm but not mean and in some of the lesson he was ACTUALLY funny, acting out Hercules's bits, but I wasn't falling for it – I was waiting for his cover to slip.

Then we had another round of show and tell. Coco showed us some amazing drawings of her mythical creatures. Simon sang a song. He sort of sang it in Coco's direction – I think he has a crush on her. And then there was some time left.

"Go on, Anjali," Leyla whispered. And then she shouted, "Go on, Anjali," so the whole class heard. This was quite unlike her so I put up my hand and Mr Shutgun called me to the front of the class.

I told them the story of how I wasn't very good at maths and the "fff" and the "fff" and the "fff"s. Some of the class began to laugh but not in a mean way and then I said a teacher had said my work was rubbish (I did not look in Mr Shutgun's direction but I think that some of the other kids did) and how my mum came up with a cunning ploy to make me love maths and for us to spend proper time together and then I left it at the cliffhanger where Sons had put down the lids instead of the bases and all our lip balms were ruined. Everyone clapped, including Mr Shutgun, and then it was time for lunch.

"Anjali, please could I have a word?" he asked.

What if his cover slipped? What if he knew I was talking about HIM and he raged like Cerberus the three-headed beast in Hercules's labours?

I was scared and looked at Leyla. Leyla mouthed that it would be fine (AGAIN – unlike Leyla). As I said, she used to worry about absolutely everything even before any of it has happened – things like if it's going to rain, being late, getting told off... so if Leyla thought it would be fine, it would be fine, I told myself.

It was as if the classroom had taken a huge breath and emptied out all the children and all that was left were the empty tables and chairs, the paintings and writing on the wall that had been done months ago and a very tall teacher with a circus moustache. The "fff"s wanted to erupt but I thought about Hercules and his bravery and I stood there trying to look unafraid while I confronted Cerberus, I mean Mr Shutgun!

Mr Shutgun towered over me; he was twiddling one of the buttons on his cardigan and he must have realised that I couldn't really see him and would be having a conversation with his button so he sat down on his desk. His eyes were less scary than I remembered them.

*Don't be fooled, Anjali*, I said to myself. *Don't be fooled!*

"Anjali, your business sounded really amazing."

I nodded cautiously.

"And you learned a lot and not just about maths, I see."

I nodded again.

"The teacher you were referring to was me, wasn't it?"

I didn't know what to do. What if I said yes? Leyla would be looking through the window. It would be fine. I don't know if other kids have this and it might sound weird but this voice in my head speaks to me when it is very quiet. *Tell the truth, Anjali*, it whispered.

I looked at him and nodded.

"I can only say that I'm sorry, Anjali. It's just that I was going through..." He stopped himself.

What was he going through? A house move? A divorce? A death in the family? Mum says that these things can make adults act a bit weird.

"There is no excuse. I am very sorry," he said, looking at me.

When he said that, I wanted to cry and the tears started coming.

"I'll do my best to do better." He gulped. I think he wanted to cry too.

He sat on his desk and was very still as I stood there and it felt, well, it felt calming and I knew that he was really sorry and I truly wanted to forgive him because I know what it feels like when me and Sons argue and I say things that I don't really mean and I realise from being at home A LOT that adults can do that too and they do not know it all.

"It's really okay, Mr Shutgun. Can I go now?"

He nodded. "Anjali," he called out as I headed towards the door. "Well done on making your lip balms. You should be really proud of yourself."

Leyla was waiting for me outside the classroom and I wanted to talk to her about the Secret Baker but some of the class had come running over to me because they wanted to know what happened next and how we solved the lip balm disaster.

"I'm not sure what happens next," I replied.

Mum appeared after school, which was unusual as she lets me walk home by myself. She and Mr Shutgun had what appeared to be a long chat. Mum was doing a lot of nodding, Mr Shutgun appeared to be talking very fast and then Mr Shutgun looked relieved and Mum smiled.

"What did Mr Shutgun say?"

"He wants to buy ten lip balms."

"No way!"

"And he said he was very sorry."

# Stuff I've Learned

Hercules performed the Twelve Labours because the goddess Hera tricked him into believing that his family were snakes and Hercules then killed them. Guilt-ridden, he consulted an oracle (a know-it-all) who told him to serve the king for ten years. The king would give him tasks or "labours" to perform in exchange for forgiveness.

What I learned is that you don't have to make people jump through hoops or perform labours to forgive them. Forgiving someone can feel like a huge, big Herculean weight being lifted.

# Chapter 11
# OMG – Mrs Marston

The weekend took ages to come as Mum said I wasn't allowed to do any work with the lip balms during the week. In the meantime, she had given the lip balms (the one with the cling film lids) to more friends and family and they started placing orders. We had a total of forty-five orders so we got to work.

Firstly, I made sure that the cases were laid out properly. We measured all the ingredients correctly, concentrating very hard to make sure that it was all right. Like a scientist with a secret formula, I stirred the coconut oil, the almond oil and the beeswax, added the vitamin E and counted out the essential oils to the exact measurement. We did this three times, making them in batches of fifteen, testing them along the way to make sure that they were fine. When the lip balms had cooled off and solidified, we put the lids on them, added the labels and I have to say they looked brilliant! AND NOTHING WENT WRONG!

I decorated the brown paper bags the lip balms were going to be packaged in. They had come with some brown pegs that would hold the bag closed so I coloured those in too and when I went into school on Monday, I proudly handed Mr Shutgun his ten lip balms.

I'm not saying that he was the same as Miss Hawthorne but he was a definite improvement on the old Mr Shutgun and he didn't shout or give out detention and, on some days, it was such fun that we forgot to mention how much we missed Miss Hawthorne.

"Thank you," he said, taking the bags.

About two weeks later, Mr Shutgun asked

if he could have a word with me. He said he had given the lip balm to his great aunt. Apparently, she knew a thing or two about lip balms, having made creams and potions most of her life, and she definitely thought I had something. I was happy to hear that she had enjoyed them but I wanted to go outside and play with Leyla and then that was when he said the name Mrs Marston. Wait! Not THE MRS MARSTON? MRS MARSTON – OMG???!

"Mrs Marston who got lost in the jungles of Borneo?" I asked, excited. "Mrs Marston who travelled the world in her biplane?"

"Ah yes," Mr Shutgun replied, clearly impressed. "You've heard of her."

OMG, I just wanted to jump up and down with joy. THE MRS MARSTON tried MY lip balm and she liked it!

"What else did she say, Mr Shutgun? Could I meet her? It would be my biggest dream come true. You know I even wrote to her? Can I? Please?" Mum always says don't ask questions like that but I couldn't help it!

Mr Shutgun looked confused. "Aunt

Louisa is quite old and sometimes gets a bit confused and that might not be such a good idea. She can be a bit, well, a lot... how can I put this? Rude and grumpy. She is what is known as a recluse – do you know what that means, Anjali?"

I didn't and I didn't care if she was the rudest person in the world.

"Let me put it this way. She likes to be on her own and she doesn't like people very much."

I just couldn't believe he was related to her. "Please, Mr Shutgun, please ask her for me? I won't trouble her. I would just love to meet her."

Mr Shutgun agreed to ask her.

Every day that week, I went into school wondering if a reply had come back but Mr Shutgun would shake his head and say, "Sorry, Anjali, I have left her several messages." A week had gone by and I had given up hope. I mean, why would she want to meet me – a school kid? Anyway, it was that very day, Mr Shutgun said that he had news.

I almost fainted when Mr Shutgun said that she said I could visit her. He wrote down the time and address on a piece of paper. Beyond excited, I tried my best not to grab it out of his hands.

*SATURDAY 15.00*
*Rose Cottage*
*Mill Lane*
*Iver*
*SL0 0BJ*

# STUFF I'VE LEARNED

Dreams do come true!

# Chapter 12
# Meeting Mrs Marston

Mum drove me there. Sons insisted that he was coming too but Dad managed to distract him with an offer of ice cream and football in the park and Mendy, well, he was happy doing anything with Dad. I was nervous and kept bouncing my knee up and down and sometimes the occasional "fff" escaped, especially as we got closer to Mrs Marston's house. We drove up to a sign that said, LEAVE YOUR CAR HERE & WALK! And then another sign that read: YOU SHOULD WALK EVERYWHERE!

Mum and I continued along a small, windy, gravel path with bushes on either side so we could only see what was in front of us, which was more winding pathway. It seemed like we were on this path forever and I am sure Mum was doubting if this was the right way.

"Oh well, at least we're on an adventure!" she laughed, as we walked along.

Then out of nowhere, a little wooden gate appeared, which we opened and that led to another path and along that pathway, I could smell the scent of lavender – yes, lavender!

We turned the corner only to see… a lavender field! There were rows and rows of tall purple lavender that swayed gently in the field. We stood there for a few minutes just to take in the smell.

I know this is going to sound weird but it felt like my ammamma was there, like she had led us there to meet Mrs Marston. As we continued through the fields, there was another wooden gate and to the side of that gate was a cabbage patch! A CABBAGE PATCH, and then I was sure that Ammamma had sent us to meet

Mrs Marston. She would do something mischievous like that if she could. I looked up and then I saw it – a little cottage.

It was the most beautiful cottage I had ever seen, straight from a fairy tale. It was yellow with a thatched roof and it had pink roses that grew around the red wooden door frame and an old-fashioned bronze bell to ring.

I was finally going to meet Mrs Marston and I was so excited that I didn't believe that a bad-tempered person could live in such a lovingly cared-for home. I rang the bell. A lady, I would say she was about fifty, opened the door with a smile that could only belong to Mrs Marston. She had her hair up in a sort of ponytail and her sparkly blue eyes lit up with a smile when she saw us.

"I have been so excited to meet you, Mrs Marston!" I said.

"Oh, I'm not Mrs Marston, I'm Jenny. I help look after Mrs Marston. You must be Anjali, come in, she has been waiting for you."

To say I had butterflies in my tummy was not true; it was more like a roaring, rumbling avalanche.

"Are you hungry?" asked Jenny.

"Excited and a bit scared," I replied.

"She is a very lovely lady once you get to know her but she can't hear very well so you have to speak up."

We walked through a very old-fashioned kitchen which smelled of vanilla and cinnamon buns and then a tiny corridor; the walls were covered with drawings of plants with their Latin names and black-and-white photos of a young lady. The young lady was very elegant; in one of them she was standing by a biplane, then she was on top of a mountain and then there were pictures of a jungle. This must be Mrs Marston when she was young. Jenny led us to the sitting room.

"Don't forget to speak up," Jenny reminded me again.

And there she was, the famous Mrs Marston. She glanced at us, scowled and looked down. I have to say my first impression was that she looked old and mean and she was not the cuddly grandmother figure with glasses and a bun that I had imagined in my head. Her hair was in a sort of bob. She had pale white skin and brown eyes, and on her lap there was no knitting

(this is what I'd imagined) but a laptop. She closed her laptop shut.

"You, like everyone else who has ever visited, want my secrets, I suppose!" she growled.

*Secrets,* I thought. *What secrets?*

But instead, I politely said, "Hello, Mrs Marston. I am Anjali and this is my mum."

Mum has taught me to be polite no matter how rude a person is. Mum smiled at me proudly.

"I don't really care," she answered. "If you don't want my secrets then what do you want?"

"Well," I began.

"Don't stand around hovering over me like a bad smell." She waved her arms at Mum. "Take a seat, take a seat." She pointed at an old, blue velvet sofa.

We sat down and seemed quite far away from her.

"Well," I continued, speaking loudly, "I have read a lot about you and the amazing things you have done and I wanted to come and meet you. I brought you this. This is the latest one."

I jumped off the old sofa and handed her my handmade vanilla and lavender lip balm.

She looked at it, made a weird face and put it to one side.

"Mum and I try to make it better each week depending on what people tell us. In the first batch, some people said it wasn't smooth enough and so we added more coconut oil. In the second batch, people asked us to try less lavender."

Even though she didn't answer, I knew she was listening because I saw her nodding.

Nobody said anything for quite some time. Eventually, Mum said, "Anjali, I'm sure Mrs Marston has things to get on with. I think it's time to go."

Why do adults do that? Mrs Marston clearly had NOTHING to get on with and we

117

had just arrived and she'd said I could come so she must have wanted to see me too.

When Ammamma was younger, she said she once had a dog who would snarl at everyone but when everyone went away it was the gentlest, kindest dog. It's just that it had been mistreated by its previous owner so it didn't really trust people until it got to know them. I'm not saying Mrs Marston was mistreated but maybe it took her time to trust people.

*Anjali, be brave*, I said to myself. *You might never get this chance to visit her again.* So I took a deep breath and, in my loudest voice, asked, "Could I have a vanilla and cinnamon bun, please? They smell very nice." I looked at her teacup. "And I'm sure they would go well with that tea. Is it camomile?"

She looked up.

"Jenny, Jenny," she shouted.

Jenny came running in.

"Jenny, did you tell this child you were baking vanilla and cinnamon buns."

"No, Louisa."

Mrs Marston peered at me curiously.

"Annie. How did you know it was camomile tea?"

"It's Anjali. My name is Anjali. I can smell it. You also have an orange and chocolate cake baking in the oven."

Mrs Marston's eyes suddenly lit up. "Bring the buns and the cake, Jenny. Sit down closer to me, Annie. I can't hear properly sometimes."

"Anjali," I repeated.

She gestured for me to pull up a chair. I sat beside her. She smelled of lavender and clove and a musty smell which I wasn't sure what it was – no offence, but it could have been the smell of an old cupboard.

She took the tin of lip balm from the table and put it on her lips and then she smiled.

"Yes, you have something." She turned to Mum. "Mrs, Mrs Anjali's mum, why don't you help Jenny bring the tea."

Ordinarily, Mum doesn't leave me with strangers but I suppose she did a risk assessment and thought that an old lady wasn't dangerous. I looked at Mum.

"Okay, I'll be back soon," Mum replied.

"You have the gift, Anjali. The gift of smell. Believe your nose. You will know when something doesn't smell quite right and when something doesn't seem quite right. Your lip balm smells heavenly. You need a floral scent that is grounding and calming. I would use a hint of geranium."

"What's 'grounding'?" I asked.

"Makes you feel safe. It connects you to the earth."

I had so many questions for her but above all, I wanted to ask her how she got lost in the jungles of Borneo.

"Mrs Marston. I wanted to know how you got lost in the jungles of Borneo and if the story is true, that you were nearly eaten by tigers."

"I don't really want to talk about that," she said abruptly, as if closing a fairy tale shut.

"Tea and cake," Mum announced as she walked in.

Jenny laid down the cake and the cinnamon buns and Mrs Marston said nothing more and that scowling look came back on her face. I would say she pretended as if we were invisible. I wanted to show her that we weren't invisible so I spoke to Jenny, telling her that the buns and the cake were probably the best that I have ever tasted.

I thought Mrs Marston had dozed off but she shouted, "My recipe."

It was time to go, and you know that when there is that awkward silence and also when Mum does that weird stare thing. I have to say I was upset because, well, I felt a bit disappointed. I knew that there was more to Mrs Marston than a grumpy, old lady but I just thought, *Be grateful, Anjali, that you met her*.

We thanked Jenny and Mrs Marston, who continued to ignore us, and just as we were about to leave the sitting room, Mrs Marston asked, "Do you think you will visit again?"

"Yes!" I smiled.

She looked back at me and I am sure I saw her smile.

Mum and I walked back down the path. "Are you sure you want to visit again?"

"Yes, Mum. Mrs Marston told me to follow my nose and my nose said 'definitely'."

Mum sighed. "Well, yes, I suppose she's a lonely old lady and some company might cheer her up."

We got into the car and drove home.

# Stuff I've Learned

People are not what they seem and, sometimes, you have to give them a chance. But if your nose (or any other part of your body, like your gut or your heart) says "no way", then you absolutely must not!

# Chapter 13
## Some Of Mrs Marston's Secrets

From then on, every Saturday afternoon at 15.00, I went to have tea with Mrs Marston. At first, she would say very little and it would be me who would do most of the talking. I would tell her about the lip balm sales and how Mum and I would spend most of our Sundays making them and then tell her all the things that continued to go wrong, like forgetting how many drops of oil I had put in. I would see a little smile emerge from the corner of her mouth like those things had happened to her too. I told her that I still wasn't happy with the little tins that we were using because they couldn't be recycled and that the cardboard boxes were flown in from America and that wasn't good either. It was when Mum and Jenny went into the kitchen that she would help me with answers.

"Ask your customers to send you the tins back so you can reuse them. Give them a discount if they do this. Yes, do this until another solution appears. If you are looking for an answer, it will appear – just make sure you ask good questions!"

Sometimes, I would tell her about Ammamma and how I missed her and how I thought she and Mrs Marston would have been friends because Ammamma was a chatterbox and made friends with anyone and she loved plants too.

Other times, Mrs Marston would let me into her world of adventure and tell me what happened to her on her trips.

The tribesman that found her in the jungle, after her biplane crashed, carried her into his village; she was almost dead. I wanted to ask her what that felt like but I thought if I interrupted her she would stop talking. She fell into a deep sleep, only once awoken by a horrible death-eating smell which she would discover later to be a flower – the rafflesia flower. I held my breath as she described it to me.

"The rafflesia is the largest flower in the world and it smells of a dead body. It absolutely hates sunlight and loves the darkness, it is poisonous and looks like a giant flowering toadstool. It can grow up to a metre in diameter and takes about nine months to bloom and then only lasts about a week and, as I said, when it flowers, it smells like a dead body."

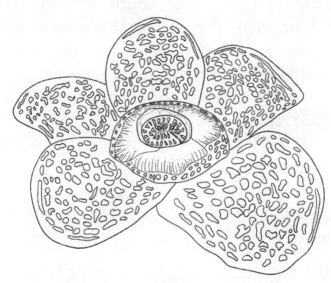

*Is it a man-eating plant?* I wanted to ask but I didn't. The village elder began a ceremony to ask the flower to heal Mrs Marston. He took the flower to her (that was the awful smell she smelled), asked for permission and it said yes. I don't know how it said yes. It didn't talk, but she said the elder knew how to communicate with the plants and flowers. I had so many questions but I couldn't interrupt her.

He then boiled the flower and made a tea for her to drink so her fever would come down. She could not drink it, so he took a cloth, dipped the tea onto the rag so drops of the tea fell into her mouth. With the rest of it, he made a paste and covered all her wounds. He did this every day while some of the village women sang to her.

"That's why it's important to sing or play music when you make your lip balms, Anjali. You are working with resonance and frequency."

Now she had lost me and I had no idea what she was talking about. So she tried to explain to me...

126

"Everything is energy and is vibrating at a high frequency – let us call this happy – or a low one, which we call sad. When you are making the lip balms, try to put happy feelings into it and so this is what people will feel when they use it," she advised me.

It was true: once we made a batch when Mum and I had argued and I tell you, nearly all of those lip balms came back to us with something wrong.

"I used to sing, dance around or play music when I first started with my creams." Mrs Marston smiled, remembering. I imagined a young Mrs Marston dancing around with a wooden spoon in her hand.

"Exploring the world and making things was when I was at my happiest, Anjali." She grinned.

"Did you want to stay in the jungles of Borneo?" I asked.

"Yes. It was a very simple life. It took me six months to get well properly and one day, I said, *Louisa, it's time to go. You know you have to move on*, and so I left with the help of one of the villagers in the early morning so I didn't have to say my goodbyes. I don't like saying goodbye, Anjali. I just prefer to leave."

"And then what happened?" I tried not to ask but I couldn't help myself.

"I came back to London and set to work on the recipes at night because, during the day, I had to go to work."

"What did you do?"

"Well, I worked in a department store in the beauty section and I did this so I could see what customers were buying and then when I got to know a few of them, I asked them to test my products and after a while, they just wanted to buy my products. The manageress found out what I was doing and I got fired."

"Fired? Fired?" I wasn't quite sure what this was.

"I lost my job," she explained, "but one of the ladies who was a customer said she would give me some money so I could work on my creams and potions all day long and it was marvellous. Things started taking off and by word of mouth, I began getting more customers. Back in those days, nobody was making products like mine and after another year, I made three times more than what I made in the department store, but I have to tell you, it wasn't ever about the money for me. It was about making.

"Then I met a man called Henry and, well..." She stopped. I could sense this was an interesting part and I wanted her to talk so I kept very silent.

"And well, you know, you fall in love but I didn't want to get married, and then..."

She stopped again. Mum sometimes does that when we are watching something on television and she thinks it's not appropriate, like people going to kiss; she just presses pause, fasts forward and says, "We'll just skip this bit."

Mrs Marston continued, "Let's just say Henry wasn't who I thought he was."

Who was he? What happened? "What do you mean, Mrs Marston?" I asked quietly, not shrieking as I wanted to do. I thought shrieking wasn't the right way to go for an answer.

"Well, at that point the business was really successful and he stole all my recipes and sold them to another company."

I gasped. So this Henry man basically pretended to fall in love with her so he could steal her recipes?

And then my mum came in and said it was time to go and I had to wait a whole week to find out what had happened. This was yet another cliffhanger!

"No!" I wanted to shout. But instead, I politely said goodbye to Mrs Marston because my mum was watching me and counted down the days to when I would see her again.

This is what I managed to piece together when I saw her the following week (she was doing that thing that adults sometimes do – tell you something but don't really tell you much):

Henry had taken all her money and left Mrs Marston heartbroken so she sold whatever she had left and decided to explore more of the world because, she said, her heart had shrunk and the only way she felt that it would get bigger was if she travelled. She sold everything she owned and bought a one-way ticket to South America where she ended up living with a tribe in Bolivia.

In Bolivia, she found out how women used mud packs made from white clay and how they would grind nuts from trees and use the oil which they put on their skin, or they would make pastes with it or boil the leaves up to make remedies (I think this is sort of a homemade potion); it was the same thing she'd found when she went to Borneo. They always had ceremonies to thank the plants for what they had given and asked the plant permission to be able to use it. She kept talking about a tribesman – he was a warrior called Shori, and every time she spoke of him, her eyes lit up. Maybe she fell in love with him? I tried to ask more about him but she quickly skipped this part and there was no way I could bring her back to this subject.

"Anjali, some things are private and you must not pry." To pry, I later discovered, is to ask too many questions about someone's personal life. Anyway, I think she had to make a choice about staying with the tribe forever or coming back to England to share what she had learned and she chose to come back and share what she had learned.

"You see, I had to let people know about nature and all the wonderful gifts it has to offer and to stop them cutting down forests, and I also wanted to show them what wonderful plants and herbs we have in our own garden."

So she set about writing books (including the one that I read with my dad) and she found a new home back in England in a forest.

She built her business up again from scratch, using only natural ingredients, and then after thirty years of caring for it and building it, she sold her company for millions to a bigger company but she kept her most important secret recipes and the things that she had learned and they were locked away somewhere safe. Mrs Marston then gave away her fortune to help reforestation (replanting forests all over the world).

I mean, WOW! I had so many more

questions. I wondered where the secrets were and what happened to the warrior man she said goodbye to. "It's difficult to say goodbye, isn't it, Mrs Marston?" I told her about how much I missed Ammamma.

A tear rolled down her cheek. "It's always difficult to say goodbye, Anjali. I don't like goodbyes. I just prefer to leave. I knew I had to leave the forest as there was something bigger for me to do."

"And then what happened, Mrs Marston?"

"Anjali." Mum came in. "It's time to go."

"But..." I would have to wait a whole week to find out.

Mrs Marston nodded and she reached out her hand to me. It was the first time she had done that. She clasped it in hers and held it tightly and I don't know why, but it made me cry.

"I can't wait until next week, Mrs Marston."

She smiled.

# Stuff I've Learned

Older people are amazing story machines. They are full of history and stories and if we stopped to talk to them, we would learn a lot!

# Chapter 14
# No More "Fff"s

On Sunday, I asked Mum if we could play classical music when we made lip balm. I hadn't really listened to classical music before. Mrs Marston had given me a list and she suggested starting with Beethoven. We had learned a bit about him in school – I think he cut off his ear for some reason – no, forget what I just said, I think that was a painter. Anyway, I had never really listened to classical music because I thought it was for, well, you know, older people. But I took out her list and the first thing on it was "Moonlight Sonata" so we put that on and WOW, it felt calming and soothing. I imagined all the ingredients growing in all the different parts of the world, the coconut oil from India, the lavender that grew in the French fields and the vanilla pods that gave off the fragrance (I'm not exactly sure where they were from) and there was a magical feeling when I began mixing them all together. Music was the missing ingredient because, from that day, our sales started to increase and Mum said that we had made enough money that I could get a website done.

Mum also said it was time to do things properly and she would set up a company and deal with all things that adults have to do when running a business like getting an accountant (this is a man who deals with all the money side and to make sure you pay all your taxes – taxes sound very boring but I think basically it is money you have to pay for schools, roads and hospitals to work well!). Mum setting up a proper company was a big thing because Mum normally leaves things halfway through, so my cunning plan to get her to finish things had worked!

By the time we paid for the website and

setting up the company, we had £200 in the bank, some of which we had to spend on more ingredients so really we were back to nothing. It seemed a lot of work to have made nothing but Mum said that's sometimes what it was like: you put back what you make so the business can grow.

We also asked the customers that we knew to send back their tins and we would give them a discount – a 10 per cent discount. We started selling lip balms for £4 and that 10 per cent was 40p. So they got a 40p discount. Can I just say, I could work this out in my head and I didn't even realise that this was maths. Not until Mr Shutgun was explaining percentages.

He said it was a difficult subject and it might take us a while to understand and so as he put questions up on the board...

They looked like this:

1) What is 10% of £100?

2) What is 15% of £100?

3) What is 10% of £200?

... I could answer the questions in my head. And the reason I could do this is that we had to do it in our business, so if we made a profit, we would give 10 per cent away, or sometimes ingredients that we bought would be on sale and there would be 15 per cent off. I could do it! I could do maths without the "fff"s. Mum's cunning plan had worked!

Mr Shutgun was impressed and said well done and, after class, he had asked how I was feeling about Mrs Marston.

"I just love her, Mr Shutgun! She is pretty amazing, just the best!"

"No, I meant—" Then he suddenly stopped. "Erm."

"What is it, Mr Shutgun?"

"Well, it's just that..."

And maybe, in my heart, I knew but I pretended that I didn't because if I pretended then it wouldn't be true.

"I have to go, Mr Shutgun. Mum gets worried if I am not home on time," I said quickly.

"Yes, of course," he replied.

Mum does get worried if I am late, but I wanted to tell her that I had finally understood percentages. I ran home to tell Mum how I had figured it out because of her.

"Mum, Mum, I got it!" I shouted as I got in. "I got the whole point of maths." She was sitting at the kitchen table and it looked like she had been crying.

I knew.

"Juju B," she began.

I had heard the way she had said my name like that before. It was when she told me that Ammamma had died and I knew immediately.

"She died, didn't she? Mrs Marston died?"

Mum nodded.

A huge lump formed in my throat. I began to cry and I could not stop.

❀ ❀ ❀

So even though it was the start of the school holidays, we didn't make lip balm for a few weeks. I didn't want to make them when I was feeling so sad. Mum had said Mrs Marston died in her sleep and went peacefully; it didn't make things seem better. I was thinking of her and my ammamma – would they meet each other in heaven? Would my ammamma be holding the cabbage that she saved but that had killed her? Do people go to heaven old or as their younger selves? Would Mrs Marston go up in her biplane? Can they see us? These were the thoughts that went round and round in my head. Just like they did when Ammamma died. Leyla said to allow all the thoughts to come and watch them like watching cars drive by and then they would go. I suppose as the days passed there was less traffic in my head but I still had this sticky feeling of sadness.

Mum called this grief and said it can take over you sometimes when someone dies. To be honest, I didn't really feel this when Ammamma died because I thought she would come back and when she didn't, I could still hear her voice and her laughter in my head and then I met Mrs Marston and it's not that I forgot Ammamma – oh, I don't know. I'd never understood what Leyla meant when she said that there was this cloud that seemed to follow her but I knew what she meant now.

I called her up. "Leyla, what did you do with the cloud? How did you get rid of it?"

"Don't try and get rid of it, Anjali. It wants you to sit with it and then it passes."

Leyla knows a lot about this. Her mum died when she was five. I am not sure how exactly – Leyla doesn't really talk about it – but I know that she was very sick.

So I sat with it and it felt like this huge dark hole that I was scared of and I went into this hole and it was empty and dark and lonely and I cried and I cried and I must have fallen asleep crying. In the dream that followed, I could smell lavender and then I could see my ammamma with her cabbage in Mrs Marston's cabbage patch and I could hear her laughing, telling Mrs Marston about chasing it and then both of them disappeared into the lavender field. I woke up and it must have been an hour later, but I woke up feeling better. Perhaps they had really met each other wherever they were? I hoped they did because they would have a lot of fun together. I got up and went to the kitchen.

Then the weirdest thing happened: Mum was unpacking the shopping when a cabbage just rolled out of one of the bags. I mean, of all the things that could have fallen out, it was the cabbage! Of course, it could have just been a coincidence and THEN Mum gave me a parcel.

"This came for you, Anjali."

I never get sent anything so I was very excited and I wanted to rip it open but Sons and Mendy burst into the kitchen so I snuck off to my bedroom.

Inside was a letter and a gift, which was wrapped neatly. I opened the letter. It was... it was from Mrs Marston!

Dear Anjali,

I hope you are not feeling too sad. I just wanted you to know that it was so wonderful to have met you, to share my memories with you and to be able to help you. You made the last few months of my life very happy. You see, I knew I was dying. I am sorry I did not share this with you. I didn't want you to visit me because you felt sorry for me but because you still found me interesting. Lots of people don't really see old people and by that I mean they just see someone who is old and has no real history, but you, Anjali, were curious. Stay curious, along with your nose: this is your greatest gift and it will take you on many adventures.

And it is all about the adventure, Anjali, it doesn't really matter how many lip balms you sell or how much money you make, what matters is the journey you go on, who you get to meet and how this changes you. A lot of this might not make sense now but it will someday when you look back.

143

Inside the gift (if you haven't opened it already) are all the secret recipes for creams, lotions and potions that I refused to sell. I was offered a lot of money for them but some things are worth a lot more than money. I want you to have them. Keep them safe and when you are older, perhaps you will use them. Here is the set of oils with instructions on how to make them yourself one day.

In the meantime, I send you lots of love from wherever I am.

Love,
Louisa Marston

P.S.
Yes, I have travelled first class and it is pretty cool, as you might say. It felt great being rich, I could do pretty much anything I wanted, but it felt greater giving away the money because I knew I was contributing to a great cause.

She had read it! She had read my letter to her!

Did Mrs Marston know that that was the last time she was going to see me? Is that why she squeezed my hand, because she didn't like goodbyes?

I opened the box slowly. Inside were old diaries and notebooks. On the diaries, she had put yellow Post-it notes saying, Anjali, do not read until you are at least sixteen! That's the worst thing you can tell a kid – not to do something – but I promised myself I would keep them safe until I was older.

She had put an orange Post-it note that said, Start here. It had an arrow that led to a bookmarked page. I carefully turned the page.

Candle for Endings and New Beginnings, it read.

Mum and I followed her secret recipe and made two candles. One of them, we kept and we lit it for Mrs Marston and Ammamma and the other one I took to school with me.

# Stuff I've Learned

I learned about percentages and that when you love someone a 100 per cent, this love doesn't go anywhere – it carries on in a different way.

# Chapter 15
## Endings And Beginnings

Mr Shutgun announced that he would be leaving as Miss Hawthorne was coming back. Most of the class were delighted but I, well, I felt sad about this. I thought about the journey I had been on. Mr Shutgun making me feel stupid, Mum trying to teach me maths in Lockdown, our lip balm business, meeting Mrs Marston. It was true what she said: it was all about the adventure, and it probably would never have started if I hadn't met Mr Shutgun.

It was the end of the day and Mr Shutgun was cleaning the whiteboard.

"Anjali, have you forgotten something?" he

asked as I walked back into the classroom.

"I have something for you."

"Oh, Anjali. There was really no need." Even though he said that, I knew he was happy as he had a big smile on his face when I gave him his gift.

"Can you open it now?" I asked.

He slowly unwrapped the packaging.

"It's handmade. Using one of Mrs— your great aunt's recipes. It's called New Beginnings. Your aunt told me that with every ending there is a new beginning."

Mr Shutgun smelled it and I thought I saw a tear in his eye.

"It smells wonderful, Anjali. Thank you," he said, smiling at me.

"No, I have to thank you, Mr Shutgun. Really, I do."

Leyla was waiting for me in the playground.

"What did he say, Anjali?"

"He said, 'I look forward to hearing about your next adventure, because I am sure there will be one'."

Leyla smiled and I smiled back. We grabbed each other's hands and ran off to find a new adventure together.

# STUFF I'VE LEARNED

Endings are not really endings: they can be the start of new beginnings.

THE END or THE BEGINNING!

# MONSTER LIFE LESSONS
## STARTING A BUSINESS – WORKSHEETS

Wait!

You thought it was over?

# NO! NO! NO!

Now it's your turn

LET THE FUN BEGIN...

## STARTING OUT

Think about what you want to make and sell.

Use this spider diagram to brainstorm your ideas. Think about: what are you good at? What do you love doing? Can you make something that people would want to buy? Some ideas to start you off: lemonade, soap, lip balm, bracelets, cakes...

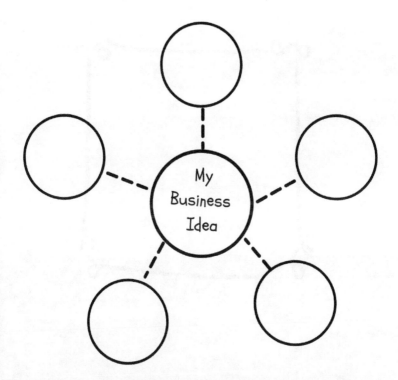

# MAKE A DECISION

1. Which idea would you like to go with?

MY BRILLIANT IDEA IS...

- - - - - - - - - - - - - - - - - - - - -

Draw it here

↓

# YOUR BUSINESS PLAN
## What do you want to achieve?

Anjali's looked something like this:

Organic Lip Balm business

1. All natural ingredients.

2. Help people have smooth lips so they don't crack and then have a problem with their "ffts"

3. Make some money and give some money to charity

4. Have fun and spend time together

## What's your cunning plan?

### Write it here

- _____
- _____
- _____
- _____
- _____

# FIND A MENTOR

This is someone who can help you. It could be a friend, a parent, a sibling, a grandparent but NOT a stranger (unless someone you know and trust is with you).

My mentor would be:

_____

Find people who have made similar things – in Anjali's case, it was Mrs Marston. If you could ask for advice, what would your top three questions be?

Write them here

1. _____

2. _____

3. _____

# MY PRODUCT

1.   What will it be made from?

_____

2.   What will it do?

_____

3.   Why do I want to make and sell this
     product?

_____

4.   Who could mentor me to
     help me make my product?

_____

# TO BE CONTINUED...

Well done for making a start – you know, the hardest part in doing anything is making a start.

If you are still inspired to continue your business adventure, you can download more worksheets at www.monsterlifelessons.com

Anjali and I would love to see your final product. You can take a picture and send it to us at:

hello@monsterlifelessons.com

We hope that you have loved this story. Keep reading to get a sneak peek of the next one in the series – Coco's Story –

# Acknowledgements

Firstly, a big thank you to the team who helped me put this book together:

Amrina Rosyada – Illustrator.

Eleanor Goymer – Editor (someone who suggests how to make the story even better.)

Rupal Pert – Teacher (Yes! I had a teacher check my work and make suggestions.)

Becca Allen – Copy-editor (someone who goes through the book line by line to make sure there are no mistakes.)

Helen Baggott – Proofreader (checks the book for any mistakes before it goes off to be printed.)

Martin at Tiger Media – Formatter (makes the book look great so it's ready for print.)

Secondly, thank you to my early readers who gave me feedback:

Janya, Ruby, Yasmeen, Pearl, Flora and 5G for choosing the cover.

To my daughter, Anjali, who inspired this story.

Lastly, to you, reader, thank you for

following us this far.

You can continue the journey at www. monsterlifelessons.com where you can download worksheets and ideas to start your own business or just say hello@ monsterlifelessons.com

Preethi

# Coming Soon..
## COCO'S STORY :
## MEETING KIBBLE

Turn the page for
an exclusive sneak peek!

# Chapter 1
# Butterfly

Mr Roberts sometimes takes us for science. He's not our class teacher and I think he used to be a scientist so science is his thing, but you wouldn't know it as he always looks really nervous. No one pays much attention when Mr Roberts is talking, probably because he is very, very tall and awkward and wears the same sweater every day and pauses a lot when he speaks. But today he was looking extra, extra nervous. Mr Roberts had placed an object in the middle of his desk and kept it covered with a piece of black material. He kept pointing to it but hardly anyone paid attention because, just before his lesson, in assembly, the date of the annual talent show had been announced. Let me explain: the talent show is a BIG deal in our school – even though Shilpa Bandera always wins with her same old Bollywood dance routine. Don't get me wrong – she's good, but give someone else a chance.

Can I just say, I'm not into talent shows. Mythical creatures are my thing. I am Coco – I am nine years old, very nearly ten.

"Settle down, please, settle down. So… yes… um… class…" Mr Roberts cleared his throat. "Did you know that a butterfly can flap its wings in, say, erm… China, and can cause an earthquake in another part of the world?"

Then suddenly, like a magician, he turned to the object in the middle of his desk, and flung off the piece of material to reveal – a beautiful, orange butterfly.

"This is known as the butterfly effect," he said proudly, looking at the butterfly and then at us.

No one looked interested and the butterfly was furiously flapping its wings in a jam jar. Butterflies are too beautiful to be trapped in jars and I was worried that it might run out of air and die. I kept looking at it bashing its pretty wings against the glass as it tried to escape.

I swear I could hear the butterfly say, "Set me free. I want to get out of here. Someone? Anyone?"

I looked around at the rest of my class to see if anyone else could hear the butterfly but none of them seemed to be bothered by its plight. Shilpa and her gang were busy pointing at Simon and giggling in the back row. Simon is the boy everyone has a crush on. I don't. I don't have a crush on anyone. I am too busy worrying about our endangered species. You know, unicorns once lived on the planet with us and now some people don't even believe they existed. I am worried that this is going to happen to the butterfly in the jam jar – that one day, people will think there were no such things as furry caterpillars who could go into cocoons and transform into beautiful butterflies.

Mark Chomsky would know that the butterfly was in danger. He was probably doing a calculation in his head, figuring out how long the butterfly had to live. Mark is the class nerd, but he didn't seem to care. I looked at Kris. Kris is a boy in our class who likes everything to be in order and when it isn't, he gets upset, but Kris didn't seem to be too bothered either.

"So," Mr Roberts continued...

I handed a note to Rita, my BFF. She would understand; she always knows what to do.

*IT'S TRAPPED. WE SHOULD SET IT FREE.*

Rita read the note, looked at me and shrugged her shoulders. That's not how she would normally act! Rita had been acting strange all morning but there wasn't time to worry about this – the butterfly needed saving. So, when Mr Roberts turned his back to write on the whiteboard, I made my way to the front of the class.

The class gasped as I took the jam jar off the table and ran. Mr Roberts turned around. "Coco, come back right now," he stuttered.

I unscrewed the top and set the butterfly free. I felt such a huge sense of relief that I didn't hear Mr Roberts shouting at me, or the children laughing. All I heard was silence as I watched the butterfly fly out of the window and I swear it stopped for a minute to look at me before it left and I'm sure it spoke to me.

"Thank you, Coco," it whispered.

"Coco. I will not tolerate such behaviour." I'd never heard Mr Roberts sound so strict.

"It thanked me, Mr Roberts. The butterfly thanked me."

The class fell about laughing.

"Stay behind after class, Coco."

I went back to my seat and Rita didn't say anything to me. Something did not feel right.

Mr Roberts continued. "So, the butterfly can flap its wings in China and cause a tornado in Mexico." Well, it shook its wings in our classroom and I could feel something strange rumbling in the air. Rita passed me a note:

*I DO NOT WANT TO PLAY WITH YOU AT PLAYTIME.*

I had to read it twice and then I thought, *Well, it makes sense as Mr Roberts has told me to stay behind.* But you know when you do that thing – pretend that nothing is wrong but know deep inside that something big is going to go down? Well, that's the feeling I really had and I felt it in my stomach.

"Okay, see you later then," I said in a really fake way as the bell went and Rita skipped past me. I don't like it when I have to pretend and I normally never have to pretend with Rita. She didn't reply.

Mr Roberts didn't shout at me. In fact, he said, he might have made a mistake with putting the butterfly in a jam jar. "Well... er... you see, I was trying to make the lesson more interesting and I came up with the butterfly idea and then..."

I looked at the clock. Break time would nearly be over and I was slightly worried about Rita's note.

"It's very difficult, you know, I mean, to keep all of you interested and I just want you to have a love of science and the world."

"I do, Mr Roberts, that's why I let the butterfly go – I didn't want it to be a mythical creature. DEAD. EXTINCT. A creature that no one will believe ever existed."

"I can see that now." He paused. "I was going to set it free and ask you all to take note of the effect that it would have on you but, er, yes, I went about it the wrong way. If you have any ideas, please share them, Coco."

"I will," I replied. "Is it okay if I go now?" I wanted to find Rita.

"Yes, of course." Mr Roberts paused again and cleared his throat. "Coco, thank you. Thank you, very much."

Adults can be weird.

Rita and I have been BFFs since reception – that's five years. We met in the Wendy house, playing dinosaurs, and have never been apart since. We have a love for:

Mythical creatures

Funny jokes or stories

White marshmallows (NOT PINK!!!!)

We have camped in Rita's back garden all night looking at the stars, eating white marshmallows and making a list of all the mythical creatures we are going to find. When we are older, we plan to explore the world together, ticking off the creatures on the list and one day, we will make a book; Rita will do the illustrations and I will do the writing. So far, we have only explored the sweet shop at the top of the hill and discovered Mr Guy – well, he is a mythical creature of sorts with his big moustache, enormous round belly and very large thumb.

Anyway, after leaving Mr Roberts, I ran to our little corner of the playground to find Rita and she was playing with – NOOOO, she was playing with Shilpa and her gang!

Okay, some quick info on Shilpa and her crew. Shilpa has two sidekicks – Anya and Misty. They hang on her every word (I am not really sure why). They love dancing – well, Shilpa loves dancing (the other two just follow). Shilpa has won the talent competition three times in a row but WE NEVER play with them because they can be really mean. But maybe Rita was desperate? Maybe she felt lonely without me?? I ran up to her.

"All sorted out. Mr Roberts even asked if we had any ideas to make the lesson interesting," I blurted enthusiastically.

My BFF then suddenly turned on me and, even worse, she began making fun of me.

"A butterfly that speaks – really?" Rita huffed.

"But it did. Well, I think it did?"

Rita turned to glance at Shilpa and her crew.

"Shilpa says believing in unicorns and monsters is for losers." There was a slight pause before she shouted, "LOSER!"

Shilpa and her gang collapsed into a heap of laughter.

At first, I had brain freeze – you know, I couldn't actually believe what Rita was saying, but then she laughed with them. "Yeah, you, you loser." She made the L sign.

I wanted to cry. Instead, I pleaded with her, "Why are you doing this, Rita?"

"Why are you doing this, Rita?" she mimicked and then she looked at Shilpa again and kicked my unicorn rucksack (the one that she had helped me choose). She left her enormous size four shoe print on the unicorn's face. I was so livid I wanted to punch her and shout, "Yeti."

The Yeti or "Abominable Snowman" is an ape-like monster who is said to live in the Himalayas. His massive footprints were found in the snow and there have been many sightings of the Yeti. Most adults seem to dismiss the Yeti as being a big bear but explorers have dedicated their lives to finding him and some have, but no one believes them.

I am going to be an explorer and prove that that the Yeti and other mythical creatures exist. I am probably going to have to do this on my own now but that's okay, well, it's not, but it will be okay.

I didn't shout back at Rita even though I wanted to, because I didn't want to upset her by letting her know that I thought she really did have big feet because I knew it would devastate her. Once, when Simon Peters laughed at the size of her feet, she burst into tears and never wore sandals again. Back then, I insisted that her feet were fine. Her feet are definitely not fine but I didn't tell her. Instead, I picked up my bag quickly so they wouldn't see my tears and ran off. When they were out of sight, I dusted my bag down and began to cry. The school bell rang and I nervously went back to class.

❁ ❁ ❁

# THANK YOU

CPSIA information can be obtained
at www.ICGtesting.com
Printed in the USA
BVHW081125121021
618737BV00009B/241